ONCE HUNTED, TWICE SHY

A Cozy Paranormal Mystery

MANDY M. ROTH

Welcome to Everlasting

The Happily Everlasting Series

COZY PARANORMAL MYSTERY ROMANCE NOVELS

Dead Man Talking
by Jana DeLeon

Once Hunted, Twice Shy
by Mandy M. Roth

Fooled Around and Spelled in Love
by Michelle M. Pillow

Witchful Thinking
by Kristen Painter

Visit Everlasting
https://welcometoeverlasting.com/

About Once Hunted, Twice Shy

A HAPPILY EVERLASTING SERIES NOVEL

Welcome to Everlasting, Maine, where there's no such thing as normal.

Wolf shifter Hugh Lupine simply wants to make it through the month and win the bet he has with his best friend. He's not looking to date anyone, or to solve a murder, but when a breath taking beauty runs him over (literally) he's left no choice but to take notice of the quirky, sassy newcomer. She'd be perfect if it wasn't for the fact she's the grand-daughter of the local supernatural hunter. Even if he can set aside his feelings about her family, Penelope is his complete opposite in all ways.

Penelope Messing wanted to get away from the harsh reminder that her boyfriend of two years dumped her. Several pints of ice cream and one plane ticket to Maine later, she's ready to forget her troubles. At least for a bit. When she arrives in the sleepy little fishing town of Everlasting, for a surprise visit with her grandfather, she soon learns that outrunning one problem can lead to a whole mess of others. She finds herself the prime suspect in a double homicide. She doesn't even kill spiders, let alone people, but local law enforcement has their eyes on her.

The secrets of Everlasting come to light and Penelope has to not only accept that things that go bump in the night are real, but apparently, she's destined for a man who sprouts fur and has a bizarre obsession with fish sticks. Can they clear Penelope's name and set aside their differences to find true love?

Jana DeLeon, Kristen Painter, Michelle M. Pillow, thanks for being awesome friends and for brainstorming to create the fun and quirky town of Everlasting. Most of all, thanks for always being there to let me bend your ear, vent, or celebrate. Love you!

Chapter One

Penelope Messing tapped her cell phone, wondering what was happening to her GPS. It had suddenly lost its mind. She sat in her rental car, pulled off to the side of a narrow road near a large lighthouse. The navigation system had been fine one second and had tried to route her into the ocean the next. The voice, which was set to a female one, had been rather insistent that she continue onward. The screen with the map displayed had very clearly shown nothing but water, but that didn't seem to matter.

The darn thing had unrelentingly told her that her destination was ahead. It even had a flag graphic shown on the display with nothing but blue surrounding it. Unless her grandfather had taken to living in a submarine and no longer resided behind his shop, in the center of town, the directions the system was giving her were faulty.

Even worse, the rental car came equipped with navigation in the dash, and it too seemed to think she needed to be in the ocean. Having two different navigation systems want to drown her was unnerving to say the least.

She pulled up the address on her phone that she'd keyed in at the airport to be sure she'd not made an error. She hadn't. This one-lane road did not look like Main Street to her. If it was, the town of Everlasting had sure downsized since she'd last been there, not that it had been a sprawling metropolis or anything before.

Prior to finding the lighthouse, all that had surrounded Penelope had been trees on both sides of the road, leaving barely any shoulder to the road at all. The dense woods had gone on for what felt like an eternity. She'd been excited when she found a structure at the end of the narrowing road. As she glanced at the huge lighthouse, she wasn't so sure it was her saving grace after all. With the heavy rains, winds and thunder booming, the lighthouse looked less like a welcoming beacon and more like an ominous warning.

If she thought she'd be able to find her way back to the airport, and to the city, she'd have already turned around and made a go for it. At least there she'd be able to find a hotel room for the night and wait out the weather. As it stood, she was committed and starting to feel as if she'd driven to the town time forgot.

Just then, lightning slashed the sky behind the lighthouse, causing Penelope to jolt upright in the car. She hit her knee on the steering wheel and winced. "Son of a bumblebee, that hurt."

On the verge of tears, she rubbed her knee, rethinking her life choices in a big way. Had she just stayed in Chicago, she wouldn't currently be lost and parked near the spooky lighthouse. Had she just turned Craig down two years ago when he'd insisted they go to dinner together, she wouldn't have a broken heart.

Frustration gnawed at her, picking away at her inner defenses like a festering wound. Everything had led her to this point, and second-guessing it all was getting her nowhere fast.

She'd wanted to get away from the city, away from her life there, away from her ex and his newly announced bride-to-be, and spend time with her grandfather. It should have been easy.

So far, the flight in had been delayed several hours due to a broken windshield wiper that wouldn't go down. Once they'd finally gotten on their way, turbulence had rocked the plane nonstop. Upon landing, she'd found out they'd lost her checked luggage, but the airlines were quick to let her know that should they locate her bags, they'd have them delivered to where she was staying. And what should have been an easy drive to Everlasting was proving to be anything but.

"You are not going to die by the creepy-looking lighthouse, surrounded by even creepier woods and an ocean that looks like it wants to swallow you whole."

Now if she only believed herself, all would be well.

I'm a goner.

As she tapped her phone, she caught the slightest of movements out of the corner of her eye. Looking up, she spotted a man in the window of the lighthouse. Maybe the lighthouse wasn't so creepy after all. Especially if she could get some help there.

Hope welled, and she considered getting out to ask for directions. If he lived here, he surely knew his way around.

That thought died the moment the man backed up from the window, and she got a good look at what he was wearing, or rather what he *wasn't* wearing—pants.

He was in a sports jacket and a pair of plaid boxers.

Nothing else.

"Oh my stars," she breathed as her eyes widened. She let off the brakes momentarily, and the car crept forward, toward the cliff side. She hit the brakes and put the car in park, needing to get her bearings and then put some distance between herself and the older gentleman wearing boxers. It was that or drive off the cliff to her death because the sight of him there was like a train wreck—something she couldn't look away from.

A series of sneezes came over her, and she held tight to the wheel, thankful she had pulled the car to a stop. Had she not, the GPS might have very well gotten its way and had her swimming with the fishes. Every bad mafia pun she could think of rolled through her head, causing a nervous laugh to escape her. She sneezed more, so hard that she nearly hit her forehead on the steering wheel.

Penelope snatched her purse from the passenger seat and took out a pack of tissues. She touched her nose with one, wondering what had come over her. Normally, she only sneezed in such a manner when she was around cats. She had a strong allergy to them and therefore did her best to avoid them whenever possible. If she didn't, she'd end up with puffy eyes and a runny nose that would last for days. Once she'd stayed at a friend's house who had two cats and her eyes had swollen completely shut. That had lasted for nearly a week and had required a shot to help clear up.

Thankfully, she had no issues with dogs and had a major soft spot for them. She'd have gotten one of her own if her lifestyle permitted it. As it was, she worked so many hours that it would have been unfair to any animal. In the meantime, she donated to animal shelters and rescue groups to help sate her longing for a furry friend. Whenever she could, she also volunteered, being sure to point out she couldn't help with any cats.

Currently, there were no cats to be seen. She sneezed more, her body begging to differ with her.

She returned the tissue pack to her purse and set her purse back on the passenger seat of the vehicle, near her carry-on bag. Her carry-on held her laptop, charging cords, and a few personal items. Having to travel a great deal for the auction house, Penelope had learned to keep a change of clothes in whatever carry-on bag she took on a flight. She was relieved she'd had the forethought to do so now, or she'd be stuck in what she was wearing indefinitely.

She adjusted her sweater that had a puppy knitted on the front of it. Her sense of fashion had always been quite different from that of other women her age, but she didn't care. At twenty-six, she wore what made her smile, and the sweater had given her the warm fuzzies when she'd spotted it in a storefront window. The leggings that she wore with it had small fire hydrants on them and paired perfectly with the sweater. At five feet nine inches, she'd had to hunt around the internet for a pair that would fit her long legs, but she'd managed to find some.

Craig, her boyfriend of the last two years, and

the man who had broken her heart into a million pieces, had hated the way she dressed when she wasn't at work. He'd mocked it every chance he'd gotten and had refused more than once to be seen in public with her until she'd changed her clothes. He also greatly disliked her sayings and refusal to say curse words. She'd always found a foul mouth to be a waste of energy. Besides, it was more fun to think of creative alternatives to words that shouldn't be said in polite company.

Craig had never agreed.

Looking back, she realized they'd never really had much in common. She loved old things, antiques of any kind, and architecture. He liked money and knocking down old buildings to make way for new ones.

They'd met while she was working at the auction house and she'd been in her professional attire. He'd come into the auction house with a friend of his who had items up for bid, and then he'd insisted she have dinner with him. He'd seemed sweet and charming, but it had all been for show. He was on the hunt for the proper wife to drag around to social functions, and she wasn't it. She wanted nothing to do with high society. She'd given him two years of her life, thinking the entire time that the relationship was going somewhere. That it had a future.

How foolish she'd been.

He'd broken up with her in an expensive restaurant, making quite the scene about how clumsy she was, how her sense of fashion was laughable and how she was book smart but would never be good wife material. He was also stuck on her lack of wanting to advance further in her career. She was content with what she did and didn't want to push onward. She made good money, more than she needed to live a modest life-style, and she liked the people she worked with. There was no reason to want more. Craig had never understood that.

Three days ago, she'd opened the newspaper to find his photo there in the engagement section with a beautiful woman smiling next to him. Within a month of their breakup, he'd not only moved on, he'd also found that cookie-cutter trophy wife he'd been so desperate for. He was living his dream, and she was in the middle of a nightmare. She'd thought she'd been in love with Craig, and that he'd felt the same for her. A small part of her had even hoped their breakup was temporary. Clearly, it wasn't. The sting of it all was still fresh enough to make her tear up.

She blinked away the pending tears. She'd shed enough of them over the man.

Within minutes of seeing the announcement in the paper, Penelope had finished off an entire apple pie and cried for several hours before getting online and booking a flight to Everlasting. So far, her last-minute trip was proving to be anything but relaxing.

"It can only get better from here, right?"

Glancing back up at the lighthouse, Penelope assumed she'd see the man in the plaid boxers once more. She didn't. He was gone from the window, and there was no light whatsoever in the lighthouse any longer. As much as she needed a helping hand with directions, she didn't want to go up to the lighthouse and ask.

She had a great-uncle who liked to walk around in his boxers as well when she was younger, and the image was still seared into her brain. At least the man in the lighthouse had gone with a nice sports jacket rather than a holey white undershirt that her great-uncle had been partial to.

Conjuring a mental image of her great-uncle, she shuddered, did a four-point turn, and drove the rental car back down the narrow road, hoping to spot a landmark or sign that would jog her memory. It had been a long time since she'd been in Everlasting. The sleepy little fishing village had apparently grown in size, at least from what she'd read on the internet.

Truth be told, she'd never thought she'd return. Her last memory of the area was of attending her parents' funeral. She'd walked silently behind the black vehicles that had held her mother's and father's coffins, her hand in her grandpa Wil's, her heart broken beyond repair. It had all seemed so confusing to her back then, like a whirl, everything happening so fast.

Her entire world had changed on a dime, and nothing had been the same. She'd been six years old then. Twenty years had passed, but it felt like yesterday. The raw emotions of it all were there, just below the surface, wanting to come out. She held tight to them, mentally reminding herself that she was no longer six years old.

She was a grown woman.

Still, the sting of it was there, floating on her memories of the time. Within hours of laying her parents to rest, she'd been whisked away from the town by her mother's parents to be raised far from Everlasting—far from Wilber Messing, her grandfather. She'd found herself in a small town in Mississippi until she'd gone off to college.

She had fond childhood memories of Grandpa Wil. He'd been attentive and caring when she was a child, always telling her one fantastical tale after another. He never ran out of interesting stories about mythical creatures and monsters that were purportedly real. He'd tell of times of old when he and his ancestors supposedly hunted these made-up creatures. He'd had a way about him that was whimsical, and that made her smile. He'd often taken her hiking in the woods on the edge of town, teaching her to track wild animals and to fish. And he'd always made her feel safe and loved.

She'd been devastated when her parents had died and even more distraught when she'd been taken far from Grandpa Wil. Her mother's parents had felt he was a bad influence and unfit to raise a small child on his own. They'd forbid her from visiting him or contacting him while she was growing up. Once she was away from their clutches, she'd reached out to him, hoping he'd want to see her once more.

He'd come right away to visit her at her university and had made trips across the country to spend time with her every year since, even after she'd gotten her master's degree and started her job in marketing. But not this year.

That was part of the reason why she'd decided to fly in and surprise him. The other part had been because of her ex-boyfriend and the rather harsh reminder she wasn't wife material in the morning paper. She'd cashed in all her unused vacation time, and she'd left the hustle and bustle of Chicago for the sleepy seaside fishing town of Everlasting.

The more she struggled to find anything that looked familiar, the more she thought she should have called first and given him a heads-up. She came to a spot in the road where she had to make a choice, left or right. She went with right and soon found herself driving down a narrow road, on a cliff side that overlooked the ocean. The storm was still going strong, so Penelope went slow, wanting to arrive in Everlasting safe, not be fished out of the bottom of the ocean by a search-and-rescue dive team.

She clutched the wheel tighter, white-knuckling her drive, as she wondered if Everlasting even had a search-and-rescue team at all. They weren't exactly a large town.

When the rain reached a rate that made it impossible for the rental car's wipers to keep up, she pulled the car to the side of the road once more, put the hazard lights on, and parked. She'd wait it out before she tried to push onward. There was no sense in risking life and limb to get there sooner. Check-in at the bed-and-breakfast she was staying at wasn't until later in the day, so she had plenty of time yet.

She wasn't sure how long she sat there before a set of yellow flashing lights came up from behind her. The lights were too bright to see what type of vehicle was there, but it was evident it was a sizeable one. Vaguely, Penelope made out a shadowy figure making its way toward her car.

She tensed, having seen one too many horror movies in her lifetime. As the figure drew closer, fear raced up Penelope's spine. The person was wearing rain gear from head to toe and walking slowly, dragging one leg slightly. Lightning rent the sky behind the figure, making them look even more ominous.

Oh boy, she thought.

Paralyzed by fear, she sat perfectly still, positive the newcomer would succeed where the GPS had failed and actually kill her. She'd end up a statistic. A footnote in a local paper.

Coming to her senses, Penelope made sure the car locks were engaged and then looked around for anything that could be used as a weapon. Much to her dismay, the only object that might work was a ballpoint pen. Still, she clutched it for dear life, her heart pounding madly.

There was a hard rap on the window, and Penelope yelped, suddenly wishing she'd taken her chances with the man in boxers. She turned her head, unsure what she'd find, but positive it would be something horror-film worthy.

Much to her surprise, she found a woman who looked to be in her mid-sixties there, tapping lightly on the driver-side window, a huge, nonthreatening smile on her face.

Penelope sighed with relief, rolling down the window.

The woman beamed. "Lost?"

"And then some," replied Penelope, releasing her death grip on the ballpoint pen.

"Where you headed?" asked the woman, a Maine accent evident.

"Everlasting," replied Penelope, ignoring the

rain that was coming in at her from the open window.

The woman laughed. "Well, child, you're in luck. You're *in* Everlasting. There was a sign down the road there. Couldn't have missed it."

Penelope's face reddened. She'd more than missed the sign. "Really? My GPS told me I had another twenty minutes. Right before it tried to drive me off a cliff into the ocean."

The woman waved a hand flippantly. "Those don't work so well around these parts. Follow my truck, and I'll get you off this stretch of road and closer to the heart of town. Tonight isn't a night for wandering."

"Thank you." Penelope barely got the words out before the woman was headed back to her truck.

They couldn't drive fast with the rain, but it didn't take long before they encountered something that looked like civilization. A small roadside fuel and service station was there, along with a hotel and tiny restaurant. Every parking space in the hotel lot was filled. Penelope wouldn't have thought of Everlasting as a tourist destination, but she was starting to wonder.

Chapter Two

There was a certain small-town charm about each of the places she drove past, following behind the woman's truck, reminding her of something from a painting rather than current times. The woman pulled her truck to a stop under the awning of the fuel station, and Penelope did the same with her rental car.

The woman was out of her truck and to the entrance of the service station in seconds, still limping as she pulled out a set of keys. She smiled wide. "You can come in here and wait out the storm, or you can head on over and get some food at the place across the way. I'll warn you, Chick-adee's is better."

"Thank you, um…"

"Jolene," she said. "And you are?"

"Penelope Messing," she returned, thankful to be out of the rain for a moment.

Jolene stiffened. "You any relation to Wil Messing?"

"I am. He's my grandfather," said Penelope with a smile. It was as she remembered, everyone knew everyone.

The woman glanced around as if she was worried someone might have possibly overheard the conversation. "Come on in, and I'll put on a pot of coffee. This storm should blow through soon enough. In the meantime, we can get dry."

Penelope followed close behind. She instantly noticed the collection of old oil cans that lined the shelves in the office. Someone had taken great pains and time to make sure every one they had was worth something. She'd sold a lot of them once a year or so ago at the auction house, and they'd done decently. There was a market for everything if you knew where to look.

"I love your collection," said Penelope, motioning to the cans.

Jolene drew to a stop in front of a coffeepot and glanced up. "Oh, those. They were something my father was into collecting when he was alive. I sort of inherited the habit when I got the shop from him." She started a fresh pot of coffee and then set about removing her rain gear. Under it all, she had on a pair of overalls and a gray sweater.

She looked like a strange combination of Lands End meets a mechanic. Somehow, it worked for Jolene.

Jolene opened the door to the cabinet above the counter area and pulled down a white box that read Witch's Brew Coffee Shop and Bakery. The second Jolene opened the box, the office filled with the sweet smell of baked goods, making Penelope's mouth water. Her stomach growled, feeling as if it were touching her spine. She hadn't realized how hungry she was until she'd smelled the delicious goodness in the box.

Jolene's eyes gleamed as she put two items on a small paper plate and brought it over to Penelope. "Here. Anna made these cranberry scones. I dare you to eat just one. It's impossible. These melt in your mouth."

Penelope smiled and then took a bite of the fluffy goodness. The flavor of nutmeg and cranberries exploded in her mouth, making her moan and Jolene laugh. They were the best scones she'd ever had.

"Good, aren't they?" asked Jolene, helping herself to two as well. She then took a seat behind a desk. Paperwork was piled high to one side. She lifted her leg and plopped her boot-covered foot on the desk unceremoniously. She ate a bite of her scone and then scowled at her ankle. "Twisted the damn thing a good one this time."

"Do you have ice? I can make you a cool compress," offered Penelope.

Shaking her head, Jolene remained seated. "Nah. I'll be fine. I twist it all the time. I broke it a good one back when I was only twenty, and it never healed right. I pretty much have a trick ankle now. Never know when it's going to go out on me or act up. I have a set of crutches I keep out back in case it gets too bad to walk on, but this is tolerable. So, you're Wilber's granddaughter?"

"I am."

Jolene looked her over slowly, a soft smile forming on her face. "You look like your momma. I should have seen that right away when I came up on you on the road."

"You knew my mother?" asked Penelope, her chest tightening. She hadn't considered that people in Everlasting would remember her parents. Their deaths had occurred when she was so young that it no longer brought tears to her eyes whenever she thought of them. Long ago she'd learned to accept the fact they were gone. She missed them and would always love them, but understood life went on.

"I did. Knew your father too. He was a good boy who grew into a fine young man. Tragic that they were taken so young. I know it broke something in Wilber. He'd already lost his wife years before, then his son, and then you were taken from him. He was never the same. Tends to keep people at arm's length now, never letting them fully in. A man can only take so much heartbreak in one life, I guess."

An awkward silence filled the room before Jolene spoke again. "Your granddad know you're in town?"

Biting her lower lip, Penelope glanced away. "No. I wanted to surprise him."

"Mmmhmm, sounds like there's a story there," said Jolene, settling into a relaxed position with her foot up and her scones in hand. "I love a good story."

With a sigh, Penelope found herself confiding in the woman. "The man I thought I was going to marry decided I wasn't good enough for him. He's now engaged to another woman."

Jolene frowned. "How long ago did the two of you split?"

"Not that long ago."

"And how long were you together?" she asked.

Penelope expelled a long, slow breath. "Two years."

"Ouch," said Jolene. "He sounds like a jerk. Good riddance to him. His loss is our gain. We've got plenty of eligible bachelors here in town."

Penelope gasped. "Thank you, but I'm not really ready to start dating again. The sting of it all is still too fresh. I only just saw that Craig was engaged several days ago. Certainly didn't take him long to move on from me."

"Honey, it shouldn't take forty-eight hours to realize he's a loser," said Jolene in a way that left Penelope smiling. "There. That is better. Now, let me think. Who would you be best with?"

Penelope took another bite of her scone as Jolene touched her cheek, deep in thought.

Finally, the woman pointed. "I've got it. Hugh Lupine. Now, he's a bit rough around the edges, but that isn't anything a good woman can't iron out. His bark is worse than his bite, and that's saying something. He's a big, strong man. Looks like those men you see in pictures that make all the women around sigh and look dreamily at them. Once a month he'll vanish for a few days, giving you time to yourself. And he'd be perfect for you, since it's clear you like dogs." Jolene pointed to Penelope's sweater.

Penelope choked on her scone. "Um, thank you, but really, I'm good. I'd like to take some time to just focus on me, not on a man."

"Can't fault you for that, but there is no harm in meeting Hugh. If he's not to your liking, I can set you up with Curt Warrick or even my nephew Sigmund. All are great choices."

It was pointless to argue, so Penelope resorted to smiling awkwardly instead.

Jolene glanced up at her. "Now, your grandfather will take exception with Hugh as my first choice, but my gut is saying he's the one. I'm pretty well known around these parts for my matchmaking skills. I'm rarely wrong. Hugh is the one for you. Not that loser Craig."

It was hard to argue with the fact that Craig was indeed a loser. The longer Penelope sat talking with Jolene, the less she felt devastated by recent events and the more she felt relieved. Had Craig not dumped her, she might have actually married him and then had to spend her life with him.

The idea no longer made her feel happy and content. It depressed her. A life with Craig every day? Always hearing his criticisms, always listening to how she wasn't good enough and wasn't going far enough in her career?

She shivered.

Maybe it was a blessing things hadn't worked out with him.

"Fate has led you straight to Everlasting," said Jolene.

"Fate?" Penelope asked, never being one to put much stock in the idea of the future being preordained. "I'm not sure about that. I'm just here to visit my grandpa and then it's back to Chicago for me."

Jolene eyed her slowly. "If you say so."

Penelope smiled. "I have a great job to get back to."

"We have jobs here too, you know."

"You sound like Grandpa," said Penelope. The man was always trying to convince her to give up everything in Chicago and move to Everlasting. He had big hopes she'd take over his shop for him one day. "And if fate really led me here, it's got a twisted sense of humor since my GPS tried to route me off a cliff."

Jolene let out a rather loud snort. "Those things don't work worth a damn for anyone around here. Don't take it personally. If Everlasting wanted you dead, it would have been more direct."

Odd.

"Storm should be letting up soon. How about some coffee to warm you up?" asked Jolene, making a move to stand.

Penelope hurried forward. "I'll get it. You sit tight."

Once she was done making two cups of coffee, she set one before Jolene then pulled an extra chair out from the side of the office. The chair reminded Penelope of something one would find in a school in the mid-seventies, but it served its purpose. She sat and sipped her coffee, nearly spitting it out the moment it crossed her lips.

Jolene cackled with delight. "Forgot to warn you that I like it strong."

Penelope pounded on her chest as she set the mug on the desk, fearful that if she dared take another sip, she'd lose her stomach lining.

Jolene sipped her coffee like it was the best-tasting thing she'd ever had, and Penelope just sat and watched.

"Are you friends with my grandfather?" she asked, never one to like silence.

Jolene stiffened and then set her coffee down as well. "Of sorts."

Of sorts?

That didn't really answer her question. All it did was pique Penelope's curiosity. She hid a smile as she thought back to when she was younger, and her mother would tell her that she asked far too many questions and had an overactive imagination.

Penelope grinned, deciding to spin Jolene's words back at her. "Now there is a story in there somewhere. I'm sure of it."

Jolene blushed, surprising Penelope. "At one time, your grandfather and I were an item. We were young and idealistic. We thought love could conquer all. We were fools. Our parents didn't agree with the relationship, and back then, you listened when your parents said no to something."

Penelope sighed. "That's so sad."

Jolene shrugged. "Our lives went in two different directions. A few years later your grandfather met your grandmother, they fell in love and had your father. And here you are today. See, it worked itself out in the end."

"What about you?" asked Penelope, invested in the saga now. "Did you find love?"

Jolene glanced away, unshed tears filling her eyes for the briefest of moments. "No."

"So you didn't end up marrying and having children?"

"Oh, I married. He wasn't a good man. Had a love for the bottle and a heavy hand." Jolene adjusted her foot on the desk. "He died after we'd been married two years. He drowned at sea." The way she said it didn't hold any remorse. She almost seemed pleased by the fact.

Penelope would have asked more on the matter, but there was a sharp rap on the exterior door. She nearly shot out of her seat like a skittish animal.

Jolene remained in place and glanced at the door. "Come on in!"

Chapter Three

A strikingly handsome man, who was obviously a law enforcement officer, entered the service station office wearing a uniform and a raincoat. His wet boots squeaked on the linoleum floor, sounding like a rubber ducky in the hands of a sugar-high toddler. He had on a large hat with a rain cover on it as well. A star-shaped badge could be made out through the rain cover on the hat. The cover itself reminded Penelope of a shower cap. It nearly made her laugh.

The man had skin that looked to be tanned all year round and was clean-shaven, showing off his good looks. The slightest hints of black curls peeked out from under his hat, and Penelope found herself raking her gaze over him slowly, admiring the show. She wouldn't mind getting pulled over if he was the one doing the frisking.

He removed the hat once he was indoors,

freeing his ear-length black hair. The action only served to up his hot factor. The man had already been up there as it was. He held the hat to his chest, the muscles in his arms flexing slightly. His dark brown eyes found Jolene. "Ma'am."

Jolene stayed in her seat. "What's got your knickers in a twist, Deputy March? You only darken my doorstep when you're on a case."

March? Darken her doorstep?

What bad b-movie did she drive into?

If there was a scuffle between the two, Penelope was putting her money on Jolene. While Deputy March was certainly good-looking and armed, Jolene had something about her that said she could be scrappy, and that she was a survivor.

March kept his hat held to his chest, his gaze moving to Penelope and then back to Jolene. "I just talked to some folks, and they said you were up near Sapphire Parker's place, and then near the cliffs, with a car none of them could recall seeing in town before."

Jolene nodded. "I wasn't near the lighthouse, but I was by the cliffs. I spotted Penelope, who was pulled over on the side of the road there. Her GPS was acting up. You know how they can be in Everlasting. What's this about? I can't see where that alone would send the town into a tailspin. Though, in this town, the gossip never ends."

Penelope remained silent as she noticed the deputy causing a small puddle of water to pool around his feet from the amount of rain he'd had on him when he entered. He'd stopped moving around, thus ending the squeaks. It was plain to see he'd been stuck out in the downpour for a length of time.

"Well, ma'am, we found two dead bodies not far from there. Foul play is suspected in the men's deaths. We're looking into all leads now and questioning anyone on what they may or may not know."

Gasping, Penelope sat up so fast that she bumped the desk and nearly spilled her coffee. She caught and steadied it, her wide eyes going back to Deputy March. "What happened?"

He licked his lower lip. "I was hoping you could tell me."

"Me? Why would I know anything about it? I don't know anything about the dead men." Confused, Penelope stared at him and realized her mouth was open as if she were trying to catch flies with it.

The look in Deputy March's eyes was one that screamed no mercy. For a split second she actually began to wonder about his age. He didn't look any older than her, twenty-six, but his eyes held wisdom in them far beyond the years on his face. "Because we got reports of you and your car in that area around what our coroner is telling us was the time of death."

Jolene snorted in a rather unladylike fashion. "March, look at the girl. Does she look like a hardened killer? She has a puppy dog on her sweater. She's what? A buck ten soaking wet? What is she going to kill? And where, exactly, were these men found?"

"The bottom of the cliffs. We're still trying to determine the cause of death, and we don't know their identities just yet." He cleared his throat. "I'm just following up on the lead, Ms. Jolene. I didn't mean any offense."

"That may be so, but I'm offended *for* her." Jolene didn't let up a bit in her firm, no-nonsense stance on the matter.

"Be that as it may," said Deputy March. The larger the puddle at his feet grew, the more his courage around Jolene seemed to expand. "I'll need to ask her some questions."

Jolene rolled her eyes. "Call Deputy August, he *lives* for the chance to play detective."

Deputy March's hard façade cracked ever so slightly, the only sign he found Jolene's comment amusing. "He does, doesn't he?"

Everlasting had deputies named March and August? What a strange town.

"Rumor has it that you were a big-city detective before you came to our sleepy little fishing town," mentioned Jolene, her gaze on Deputy March.

"Yes ma'am," he said, inclining his head.

"How long were you there?" she questioned.

Deputy March's shoulders slumped slightly before he quickly righted himself. "Feels like I've been policing things in one form or another for centuries."

"I'm sure it does," returned Jolene, something off in her voice. "Do you ever get tired of it all?"

He cleared his throat. "Ms. Jolene, any information you can provide would be helpful. Same for your friend here. Whatever she might know could help us figure out what happened to the men we found."

Penelope put her hands on her knees, nervous, though she wasn't sure why. It wasn't as if she'd murdered anybody or had anything to feel guilty over. "I don't mind answering your questions. Do I have to go down to a station or something? Should I call an attorney? Am I being arrested?"

Jolene shook her head. "For the love of pecans, no. He can ask what he wants here, and if he pushes too far, I'll take him by his ear to Sheriff Bull. Francine and I go way back."

At the mention of the sheriff, March paled. "Here is good."

Penelope felt like she was in a bad movie. The kind where the big-city girl enters a small town, only to be pulled over by the small-town officer, never to be seen again.

"Where were you tonight?" he inquired, somehow managing to ask his question while Jolene glared holes at his head.

Jolene groaned. "For Pete's sake, March. We've already established she was up near the cliffs on the edge of town. Follow along, would ya?"

Penelope wasn't sure if Jolene was helping or hurting her case. "Um, I was near the cliffs, like Jolene said. I was trying to find my grandfather's house, but my GPS tried to route me into the ocean. I was first parked by a lighthouse, and there was some guy in boxer shorts there, so I didn't want to ask for directions, plus I couldn't stop sneezing, so I turned around and tried to find my way into town. I couldn't see very well when the rain increased and the road was narrow, so I pulled off a bit to wait out the storm. That was when Jolene found me."

Jolene stared blankly at her. "You know you ramble a lot when you're nervous."

She'd been told that more than once in her life.

Deputy March pulled out a small pad of paper and a pen. "Okay, you were out by the lighthouse, and there was a guy in boxers. Can you describe him?"

"Erm, he was older, wearing plaid boxers and a sports jacket. Nothing else."

Jolene snickered.

Penelope squirmed in the chair, feeling like she was on trial for her life, and Jolene thought it was funny.

"Did you get his name?" asked Deputy March, staring hard at his pad of paper as he wrote.

Penelope blinked. Was he serious? The expression he leveled on her said he was. She swallowed hard. "No. It seemed unwise to get out of my car during a storm and go up to a stranger who was wearing only boxer shorts to have a chat."

Jolene laughed more, sipping her coffee. "She's talking about Cornelius, March."

Deputy March exhaled loudly and began scratching through the notes he'd taken. "That damn ghost. I swear he's on my last nerve. If he'd just make himself visible to men too and start wearing some pants, my life would be so much easier."

Ghost?

Penelope went rigid. Surely the man was kidding.

No one laughed.

She thought about the man she'd seen wearing boxers. He'd been real, hadn't he? He'd looked real. And she didn't believe in ghosts.

Deputy March stared at her once more. "Can anyone verify what you were doing out near the lighthouse and the cliffs?"

She stiffened as she realized he really did think

she was a suspect. In all her life, she'd never even gotten so much as a speeding ticket, let alone questioned over a murder. She was the type of person who didn't litter, didn't jaywalk, put extra money in parking meters, and who followed the rules. She didn't kill people. She didn't even kill spiders. She relocated them. They had a right to live too.

"I was lost. Jolene found me. I'm not sure what there is to verify," she said, staying calm, despite the sweat forming on her palms. Flashes of being forced to wear an orange jumpsuit and talk to her grandfather through glass came to her mind. She'd never survive the slammer. She could barely make it when her internet connection went out. A six-by-six cell and communal showers were not something she could deal with.

"Did you see two men out there?" he asked. "They were mid-thirties."

She shook her head, panic continuing to well in her. "Just the older man in the boxers."

His gaze narrowed on her. "You're telling me you didn't see anyone else out there."

"Yes. That's right. Well, other than Jolene."

He looked to Jolene. "Ms. Bails, did you happen to see anyone else out that way?"

"No," snapped Jolene, and from the expression on her face, she was done discussing it.

"Ms. Jolene?" asked Deputy March, adding a bit of saccharine to his voice.

Jolene eyed him in a way that said she wasn't having any of his questions, and she wasn't falling for his charms. "Shouldn't you be more worried about what two men were doing near the cliffs at that time of night, in the middle of a storm, than what Penelope and I were up to?"

Deputy March kept his pad of paper out. He glanced at Penelope. "Okay, you said you were headed to your grandfather's house. Does he live here in Everlasting?"

Jolene sat up so fast that she spilled her coffee, but she paid no mind to it. "I don't see what that has to do with anything."

Penelope wasn't sure what harm could come from answering the man's question. "Yes. My grandfather owns an antiques shop here in town on Main Street."

Deputy March managed to pale even more. "Wilber Messing is your grandfather?"

She nodded—and the man unsnapped the top of his holster as if he might need to pull his weapon in a hurry.

Penelope froze.

Hold the pickles.

Did he really think she a threat? Was he going to shoot her on the spot, just for getting turned around on the edge of town?

Without thought, Penelope put her hands up as a sign of surrender.

Jolene stood and limped around the desk in the deputy's direction. "March, you got about two seconds before I have Sheriff Bull on the phone. Correct me if I'm wrong but didn't the new Jack Reacher novel come out? She'll be deep into reading that and none too pleased she got interrupted because you're on a mission to ruin a young girl's life."

He stepped back from Jolene, but his gaze landed on Penelope. "Don't leave town until we get this cleared up."

His radio went off, and a woman's voice came over it. "March, you there? Templeton is on Main Street dressed in a general's costume, riding around in a shopping cart. He's scaring tourists again."

Deputy March pressed the button on his handheld. "Judy, can you send August? I'm wrapping up at Jolene's."

"Can do, sugar," the woman said, her voice raspy.

All Penelope could do was manage a small incline of her head as Jolene really did shove Deputy March out of the door. She locked it behind him and flipped her sign around to read closed. She eyed Penelope. "You can put your hands down."

She did.

"That wasn't good at all," said Penelope.

Jolene sighed. "It could be worse though. It could be Deputy August looking into it all. He's completely incompetent. At least March has a brain."

"I didn't do anything."

"I know that, but now that he knows who your grandfather is, the whole town will be hearing about it by midday. Trust me when I say you'll be guilty until proven innocent in most of their minds." She sighed. "You'd think with the amount of dead bodies we get around here this wouldn't raise an eyebrow."

Penelope's throat felt as if she'd swallowed sand. "Exactly how many dead bodies does Everlasting see?"

Jolene shrugged a shoulder. "I honestly stopped counting years ago. You mentioned that you were staying at the B&B?"

"Yes."

"It would be better if you stayed with Wil," she said. "No one would dare to bother you there."

"But they will at the B&B?" asked Penelope, her mind racing. All she'd wanted to do was visit her grandfather for a bit, and now she was a murder suspect. "I can't just impose on my grandfather without warning. I'll stay at the B&B."

"I'll call the sheriff. As soon as the storm breaks, we'll get you settled in at the B&B, but trust me when I say it will be better to stay with your grandfather. Folks around here have a healthy fear of him."

She nearly laughed at the idea of anyone fearing him. He was sweet and lovable. The biggest fear they should have was if he'd start wanting to hug them. He was a hugger. At least he always was with her.

Jolene took a deep breath and glanced out the window. "The storm is just about over. We can get you on your way to your grandfather's."

"Should I be worried that I'm a suspect in Deputy March's eyes?"

Jolene pressed a smile to her face, but it didn't reach her eyes. "No. Not at all, honey. Here, let's get you another scone. They make everything better."

Suddenly, Penelope was regretting her decision to come back to Everlasting.

Chapter Four

Hugh Lupine weaved around a large oak tree as he stepped out and onto Main Street. It was still early enough in the morning that Main Street wasn't filled to the brim with people just yet. Freak storms had blown through during the night and into the early hours of the day, leaving leaves scattered about the street, and most people hunkered down for a bit.

He wouldn't have been in the area if he didn't need to check on his friend who wasn't on his boat this morning. Captain Petey tended to vanish for days at a time. Most went with it, knowing the man was old, set in his ways, and touched in the head. Hugh thought of him as an uncle who, while certifiable, was family of sorts. He'd worry until he knew where Petey was.

If he guessed right, Petey would be sleeping off too much whiskey down at the Magic Eight Ball.

The place catered to the locals and was a watering hole that Petey frequented. Shorty, the owner, often took pity on the old man, letting him sleep there rather than making Petey head back to the marina late at night. Often Petey had company during his all-nighters in the form of Monte Gallagher and Sam Chester. The three of them were all old-time fishermen and Magic Eight Ball regulars.

Petey lived in a small cabin that was near Hugh's home. The two did their best to look out for one another. Though Petey tended to leave bottles of booze as peace offerings and wellness packs when Hugh left groceries and food for the old man.

Hugh walked quickly past Hunted Treasures Antiques & Artifacts, making sure he stayed off the sidewalk in front of the shop. He treated the area like it was lava and if he dared step into it, he'd instantly burst into flames. It was dramatic, but how he felt about the place.

The brick building was old and more than likely considered historic, as it had been there since the town was built. The storefront fit with the quaint aspect downtown Everlasting had. The green awning that was above the giant picture window, and below the sign for the shop, was always spotless. It was as if the birds were even afraid to do their business anywhere near a Messing property.

He couldn't blame them.

The old man probably had some sort of hexed

artifact in there that repelled pigeons. He'd heard all about the artifacts that called the shop home. They varied from crystal balls to end-of-the-world stones. From his understanding, the shop would give Ripley a run for its "believe it or not" money.

No thank you.

Hugh shuddered slightly as a case of the heebie-jeebies came over him. He hoped no one noticed his obvious discomfort around the shop. He'd be hard-pressed to live down the reputation of being scared of it if they did.

The place always seemed to have tourists venturing in and out, looking for a great find. While he knew the shop held more than mere antiques, he'd never been curious enough to wander in. He'd taken the townsfolks' word on Old Man Messing being the keeper of artifacts that were best left out of the hands of humans. Hugh had never set foot in the place despite having lived in Everlasting all his life, and he didn't intend to ever enter.

Giving Hunted Treasures a wide berth was ingrained into Hugh's being. He'd grown up hearing stories about the Messing family and how they'd hunted a number of supernaturals to the point of extinction.

For a brief period during his youth, he'd been neighbors with some of the Messing family. He'd even played with the little girl who had lived in the house next to his—even with their age difference.

He could still remember the look of horror on his parents' faces when they'd found the two of them playing together. Hugh hadn't understood the issue then. Why he couldn't be friends with the little girl. That had seemed like a lifetime ago.

While Wilber Messing claimed he was no longer into the old family business of hunting and killing supernaturals, Hugh wasn't taking any chances. Especially since a number of his ancestors had been victims of the Messing supernatural hunts and culling. They were famed, and stories were often passed down generation to generation, told to frighten young supernaturals and to keep them in line. As far as he knew, Wilber hadn't offed anyone in town, but a lot of strange things happened in Everlasting. And Hugh had no desire to have his pelt end up on the wall of the old man's shop.

Right now, Wilber was the least of Hugh's concerns. Currently, he was trying to artfully dodge the small, annoying man walking behind him, a glass jar in hand. The jar was nearly filled to the brim with coins and cash, and it had all been courtesy of Hugh and his mouth.

He didn't understand what the big deal was. So what if he tended to be colorful with his language? Apparently, not everyone in town liked it, and they'd suckered him into a bet with a man he hated to lose to. Now, it was a case of clean up or pay up.

And pay up he had.

It seemed as if all he'd done the last four days was pay up.

"We all heard you, Hugh," said Buster, trotting after Hugh like a stray dog, as he held out the jar more. There was no way Hugh could miss the thing, yet Buster continued to make it obvious. He shook the jar, and it barely rattled—a testament to just how many times Hugh had to use cash rather than coins because of his mouth, and the steep fines that came with certain words, along with the frequency of use.

Apparently, Hugh was a master wordsmith.

Buster smiled so wide, Hugh wasn't sure how the man's face didn't break. There were very few times in the man's life that he got to boss Hugh around. This was one of them. "Pay up. You know the rules, and you're the one who said you could do it. Now, if you want me to tell Curt that he wins the bet, I can give him a call."

There was no way Hugh was going to fold this soon into the bet. It didn't matter how hard it was for him to watch his mouth, he'd figure out a way. And then he'd make Curt eat his words.

With a growl, Hugh reached into the back pocket of his jeans, pulled out his wallet, withdrew a five-dollar bill, and shoved it into the jar. "There."

"That one was at least a ten-buck infraction," said Buster, still holding the jar out. He shook his head, as he whistled long and loud, drawing the attention of a few people passing by. "You somehow managed to string together four sentences full of nothing but foul language. I didn't even know that was possible."

"Yeah, well we all have our gifts," snapped Hugh, annoyed he'd allowed himself to agree to the bet to start with. Curt Warrick had been a pain in his backside since elementary school, and his best friend. Now that the men were in their thirties, not much had improved between them when it came to competing. If anything, it had gotten worse. Such was the way of it between cats and dogs though.

Hugh snorted.

He really hated cat-shifters.

"All the money goes to a good cause," reminded Buster.

How could Hugh forget? The entire town had seemed happy about the bet, knowing he'd never be able to win and that the coffers for the new school fund would get a well-needed boost.

Mrs. Mays walked by, wearing her Sunday best, even though it was a Tuesday. He couldn't recall a time he'd ever seen her looking disheveled. The elderly woman adjusted her large-brimmed yellow hat and pursed her lips at the sight of the jar. She lifted a gloved hand and pointed a finger directly at him, tsking as she did. Instantly, he felt five years old again. "Shame on you, Hugh. They only just started the collection and look at how full that jar is. You need to learn to mind your tongue. And I haven't seen you in church in ages. Will I see you there Sunday? Curt makes sure he checks in."

Mumbling an apology, he avoided making eye contact with her. The woman could scare the hair off a dog with nothing more than one of her menacing stares. She'd perfected the art of them several decades back, and so far, none could rival her. She'd taught Sunday school for as long as Hugh could remember and she took great pride in all her pupils growing up to be fine upstanding citizens. He didn't have to imagine her disappointment with him. It showed on her face.

It probably didn't help that she'd seen Hugh last week walking around in a T-shirt from a rock band she'd once been sure had secret messages from the dark side on their albums. He'd never actually attempted to play any of their music backward so they very well might have. He knew a few people in town who had sit-down monthly lunches with the devil, otherwise known around Everlasting as Luc Dark, so he wasn't sure what all the fuss was about. Hell, Everlasting had its fair share of residents who were demons. It wasn't as though they discriminated against any supernaturals.

They just preferred to keep humans from taking up residency. They were fine as tourists, coming in and spending their money to infuse the economy, but not with everyday, all-the-time living in Everlasting. There were too many secrets to be kept. Too many humans simply couldn't know about. The town was full of oddities and people who were more than they appeared to be. Some paid no mind to it. Others made it their life mission to help keep it all a secret.

None of that changed Mrs. Mays's views. She'd drag the devil himself into church by the ear if given a chance. If the devil knew what was good for him, he'd keep away from Mrs. Mays.

Once she was down the street, Hugh focused his attention on the small man near him. At six-five, he towered over Buster, and he already knew alpha poured off him in waves when he was upset. Buster could no doubt feel the power. Hugh shoved another five into the jar, only barely managing to hold in another growl.

Buster's grin faltered. His hair was receding, and he was thick around the middle. He was a few years younger than Hugh but managed to somehow look at least ten years older. As far as Hugh knew, Buster had never had a girlfriend, or any love interest for that matter, but he strongly suspected the man had a thing for the secretary at the high school. He'd seen him fidgeting with his bow tie whenever the woman was around. Buster brought attention to his spare-tire waist by wearing sweater vests that were two sizes too small, and plaid shirts with bowties.

Nothing about the man was stylish. To each his own.

"The fund for the new middle school thanks you," said Buster.

It was on the tip of Hugh's tongue to tell the man exactly what he thought of the school fund, but that would probably cost him several hundred dollars in fines, so he went with a rather threatening smile and watched as sweat broke out on Buster's brow.

"Don't eat me," said Buster, swallowing hard, pushing his glasses up his nose with one hand, while holding the jar with the other. It began to wobble.

"What will eating you cost me?" asked Hugh, stepping closer. He glowered down at Buster. "Bet it's cheaper than what I've paid so far, and I'm only four days into my month-long cursing ban."

Buster paled considerably, and his nose began to twitch. A sure sign he was starting to lose control of his animal side. When Buster squeaked, Hugh knew he was on borrowed time.

Glancing around, Hugh hoped Main Street wasn't full of tourists, as it normally was this time of day and year. The annual Cranberry Festival always meant an explosion in population, at least for the month of October in the tiny Maine seaside town. For as much as they liked the money tourism brought to the area, it was certainly interesting trying to keep the town's secrets under wraps with so many humans roaming around with cameras hanging around their necks.

The residents of Everlasting wouldn't be able to easily explain away how a mild-mannered accountant up and shifted shapes into a giant rat in the middle of the street. No. That wouldn't be something a cover story would do much for—though Everlasting had some of the best cover-ups around. Already this morning he'd seen Templeton, a local known for his eccentric ways, riding down Main Street in a shopping cart, dressed as if he were a general and the cart his tank. Everlasting didn't need anything else happening in broad daylight.

"Calm down, Buster," said Hugh, reaching for the man, only to have him lurch back, his nose twitching faster. "I won't eat you."

Right now, thought Hugh.

Buster hugged the jar to his chest as if it would somehow protect him should the alpha male shifter have a change of heart about eating him. "You never know when it comes to *your* kind."

By "your kind," Hugh knew the man meant wolf-shifters. He didn't take offense. It was the truth. One didn't ever know if his kind would decide to eat them. Wolves were notorious for their tempers.

He shrugged and was about to comment more when the hairs on the back of his neck rose. His wolf pushed upward with a speed that nearly caught him off guard. He snarled and had to fight to push it down. A big rat would be hard to explain, but a huge wolf would be even more so.

Hugh wasn't sure what prompted his wolf's outburst. The last time he'd suffered a bout of uncontrolled wolf issues had been puberty, and he certainly hoped he wasn't going through a version of that again.

Buster's nose twitched again as sweat dripped freely from the man. The armpits of his shirt were soaked. It was early October in Maine. Sweating wasn't something many people did that time of year.

Hugh caught the man's arm and tugged him closer. "Stop."

"You're the one making noises like you're changing your mind about eating me," managed Buster, his voice barely above a whisper. The smell of his fear called to Hugh's wolf, making it want to come out and play. "I've been told my kind don't taste very good."

Hugh arched a brow, and a lecherous grin eased over his face. "You sure? I'm betting you taste like chicken."

Buster gulped.

Hugh snorted and then paused. It was almost too easy getting the small man riled. "Wait. What do you mean I was making noises like I was going to eat you?"

"A second ago, you made a noise that suggested

you were about to lose control," said Buster, still clutching the donation jar as if were a lifeline.

Huge debated on telling the man that the jar would do little to stop him if he did decide to eat him. Sensing Buster was close to wetting himself, Hugh left well enough alone. He took a step back, wanting distance between him and Buster. Lifting his hands in the air, Hugh tried to appear nonthreatening as he walked backward more. "Listen, I promise not to eat you if you promise to stop waving that…awesome…jar in my face."

He'd nearly slipped and cursed again.

Buster's eyes widened a second before the sound of squealing tires filled the air around them.

Chapter Five

One second Hugh was standing on Main Street and the next he was flat on his back, lying in the middle of it, positive someone had hit him with a ton of bricks. He mumbled what he thought on the matter and looked up to find Buster above him, holding the jar out, a knowing look on his face.

"That is going to cost you big time," said Buster, seemingly unconcerned with Hugh's well-being as he rattled the jar once more.

With a groan, Hugh attempted to sit up but was shaken and needed a moment to get his bearings. "What the...?"

"Hold the pickles!" yelled a voice that sounded like an angel.

A face that matched the sweet-sounding voice appeared above him. The woman had high cheekbones and a narrow nose. Her lips were full, and she had a deep cupid's bow, making him instantly wonder what her lips would feel like pressed against his. A pair of royal-blue eyes that reminded him of the ocean before a storm stared down at him as a mass of dark brown hair fell forward, nearly eclipsing the woman's face entirely. The woman was so beautiful that Hugh blinked, confident he'd died and gone to the great beyond.

If it weren't for the throbbing pain in his legs, he might have really believed he was dead and an angel was above him. Then again, he wasn't so sure he was destined for the pearly gates.

She grabbed her long hair, wrangling it into a self-contained loose bun. She was already on the pale side, but he watched as the color drained from her beautiful face. His gaze naturally eased down the front of her to her breasts, and he drew a brow up at the sight of a puppy dog knitted on her sweater. That certainly wasn't what he was expecting to find the hot goddess wearing. It looked like something no one out of elementary school would entertain putting on, yet the woman wore it well. It hugged her every curve. Hugh's body responded in kind, making his jeans feel extra snug in certain areas.

The longer he stared up at her, the more he realized just how fast his heart was pounding. Her full lips were moving, but he heard nothing over the sound of his own heart beating madly. It was on the tip of his tongue to do something stupid and ask the woman to marry him. He was about as far from the marrying type as a person could get. He was all about no commitments and no strings when it came to dating, but this beauty was one his wolf, and his man side, seemed to want to mark as theirs.

That freaked him out.

Reaching up, he touched her cheek, needing to make contact with her. As he did, her hand moved over his, her lips still moving, a frantic look still covering her face.

"How badly are you hurt?" she asked.

It took Hugh a moment for his head to catch up with the words. When it did, a lopsided grin spread over his face. "I'm good. What happened?"

"You walked right out in front of me," said the woman. "I tried to stop my car, but I wasn't fast enough. I hit you with my car."

That explained the pain. As a shifter, he'd heal quickly and could take a great deal more physical injury than a mere human could. Nothing explained his need to propose to the woman on the spot though. That was still a mystery to him and much more worrisome than being hit by a vehicle. None of it explained the giddy feeling that was spreading over him at the sheer closeness of the woman.

Buster pushed the jar between Hugh and the woman. "You'll live. Now pay up, Hugh."

With a growl, Hugh sat up faster than someone

who'd just been struck by a car should have. As he glanced at the vehicle in question, another round of words that would cost him a pretty penny fell out of his mouth. It wasn't bad enough he'd been foolish enough to walk out in front of a moving vehicle; he had to do so in front of a hybrid one. Curt would never let him live it down. By the end of the day, the town would be gossiping that he'd been cut down by a golf cart. The grapevine tended to do that to a story.

The beautiful woman pushed Buster aside and touched Hugh's shoulder, causing heat to flare through his arm. He gasped and hoped she didn't notice the effect she was having on him.

She bent more. "I hit you pretty hard. I should call an ambulance. You need a doctor."

He stifled a laugh. What he needed, she'd more than likely not want to give on the spot. "Like Buster said, I'll live."

She gave Buster a hard look, causing the man to back up. He clutched the jar to his chest once more, appearing worried. "He needs to be seen by a medical professional," she said, as if daring Buster to contradict her.

Buster gulped.

Hugh felt for the small man. The woman, while breathtaking and wearing a puppy dog sweater, still managed to come off as threatening. The wolf in

Hugh seemed pleased, as if it recognized a bit of alpha in the female.

Hugh pushed to his feet and winced as pain lanced his right leg. It had probably broken during the accident but was on the mend already with his accelerated healing abilities. "I'm fine. Really."

She rounded on him, and he realized Mrs. Mays had nothing on this woman and her ability to strike fear in those around her with nothing more than a hard look. How could someone so beautiful look so deadly? "What are you doing standing? You were just hit by a car!"

He snorted. "That's hardly a car. It's a hybrid. Like a mosquito bite or something."

The woman's eyes widened, and she took a small step back. "I think you're in shock."

"I think you're beautiful," he blurted. "Have dinner with me. Wait. What time is it? Have lunch with me."

Buster laughed and tried to hide it behind a cough.

"Hugh, what in the world are you doing out in the middle of the street, holding up traffic?" asked Jolene Bails, her head out of the window of her pickup truck as she pulled to a stop behind the car that had struck him. Jolene glanced at the angel near Hugh and smiled wide. "Penelope, I see you've met Hugh. He's single. Same as you. Snatch her up, Hugh. Quick before someone else does."

Penelope blushed, and Hugh nearly did the same. Jolene had always been something of a mother figure to him as he'd lost his mother when he was very young. Rumors surrounding her death had always linked it back to the Messing Hunters, but Hugh never had any hard facts to back it up. Just a lot of small-town gossip.

Jolene scowled as a sheriff's car pulled up behind her truck. When Deputy Jake Majoy, better known as March, got out, Jolene cast a worried glance in the direction of Penelope.

A spike of unwarranted jealousy went through Hugh, as the deputy set his sights on Penelope. He and Jake were friends and he'd never been jealous of the man before.

As Penelope noticed the man, she tensed.

"I got a call about a hit-and-run," said Jake.

Hugh snorted. "What busybody phoned that in?"

"There was no hit-and-run," said Penelope. "There was just a hit-and-stay. I was driving, under the speed limit, and all of a sudden Hugh stepped out into the street. I clipped him with my car."

Jake whipped out a notepad and began writing, looking up at random to give a speculative glance at Penelope. Strangely, Hugh felt the need to step partially in front of her, putting himself between the woman and the deputy.

"So, she struck you with her vehicle?" asked Jake.

"I stepped out in front of her, so yes. But not hard," Hugh said quickly. "It wasn't her fault."

"Well, it was kind of hard," said Penelope, her face now very red.

Jolene snorted loudly from her truck. "March, stop trying to make the poor girl out to be Norman Bates. There was no crime here. And clearly no hit-and-run. Just a hit-a-Hugh, and he's fine. Look at him."

"Yep, fine," said Hugh, putting his arms out wide for the man to see.

Buster grinned. "And he's clearly smitten with her."

Smitten? Who actually said that anymore? Hugh glanced at Buster and groaned.

Jake stood rooted in place, narrowing his gaze on Penelope. "Miss, you've been in town less than a day, and already you're tied to two dead bodies and have hit a local with your car. I'm almost afraid to see what you'll do before lunchtime today."

Hugh tensed. Two dead bodies?

Who was dead now?

Everlasting had to have one of the highest per capita murder rates in the state. That had a lot to do with the fact they were full of supernaturals, and murder and mayhem sort of came with the terri-tory. It was really hard to have this many shifters, vampires, and magics in one spot and not have someone end up dead.

Still, he couldn't believe the heavenly beauty before him was linked to two deaths. She was still so worked up over hitting him with her car that he was worried he'd need to get *her* medical attention.

"As Jolene said, there was no crime here," warned Hugh. "If anyone should be in trouble here, it's me. I'm the one who walked right out in front of her."

Buster gasped. "Is it me or did Hugh just accept responsibility for something, while avoiding cussing, and did anyone else catch the way he keeps looking at the young lady? Smitten, I tell you. Smitten."

Hugh set his sights on Buster, and a low growl began to emanate from the back of his throat. In a flash Buster was sweating again, appearing nervous.

Jolene laughed. "It wasn't you, Buster. Hugh knows a good thing when he sees it."

Jake stared past him at Penelope. "Ms. Messing, remember what I said about leaving town. And try to stay out of trouble. You're setting a new town record, and you've been here less than four hours."

Messing?

Hugh's gaze went to the antiques shop and then back to Penelope. No. She couldn't be related to Wilber. As he stared harder at her, a sinking feeling started in the pit of his stomach. He let out a line of expletives that instantly had Buster holding the jar out before him. "You have got to be kidding me! I was run down by a hunter, and you want me to pay for it?"

Jake perked. "So she did hit you with her car intentionally?"

"No," Penelope said quickly. "I'd never do that. And what did he mean by a hunter? I don't hunt. I hate the idea of killing poor defenseless animals. In fact, I'm a borderline vegetarian."

Hugh stared at her. Was she joking?

Chapter Six

Penelope waited for Hugh to tell the deputy once more that she'd not purposely struck him with her car. That he'd walked out in front of her. As Hugh's amber gaze slid over her and widened, she gasped. Did the man suddenly think she really had hit him intentionally?

"Hugh walked out in front of her," said the short man in a sweater vest, holding a jar that had Hugh's name on it. "She didn't aim for him or anything. Though let's be honest, Hugh could stand to be run over."

"Shut it, Buster," said Hugh, still watching her as if she were the devil. He certainly didn't look as if he still wanted to take her to lunch or dinner.

Buster ignored Hugh and offered Penelope a sheepish smile. "I like your sweater."

"Thank you." She gnawed at her lip and tugged

lightly at her sweater as nerves got the better of her. So far, her last-minute trip to Everlasting was a complete and utter disaster. Her bags were more than likely in another state or country. The GPS had tried to run her off a cliff and into the ocean. And if that wasn't enough to make the trip anything but enjoyable, a hunk had walked right out in front of her car and was now acting as if it was her fault he didn't know how to use a crosswalk or look both ways.

"Do they have a version in a sweater vest with a poodle on it?" the man with the jar asked.

She glanced briefly at him, wondering if he was serious. The expression on his face said he was. "Um, I don't think so."

"Drats." He snapped his fingers. "I really like it."

Deputy March moved closer to her, accusations strewn across his face. He thought she was guilty, and he didn't bother to hide as much. "I need to see your license."

This cannot be happening.

With a grunt of frustration, she came to the understanding that this wasn't a nightmare, she wasn't dreaming; Everlasting was proving to be the worst possible place she could have picked to relax. "Yes, of course. Anything you need, Deputy. I swear I didn't aim at him or anything. He just stepped right out in front of me." She turned to go for the rental car to retrieve her purse.

"Enough, March," snapped Jolene, peering at the deputy shrewdly. "Stop trying to make the poor girl out to be a member of the Manson family. You're like a dog with a bone. No offense, Hugh."

"None taken," returned Hugh with an indifferent shrug.

"Jolene, let me handle this," pleaded Deputy March. "Penelope keeps popping up in the wrong place at the wrong time. You have to understand my concern."

"She's a sweet girl." Jolene pointed at the deputy. "And don't you go claiming otherwise."

"She's a Messing," offered Hugh with a huff. It was clear he had great issues with her last name, though she wasn't sure why. Her grandfather was incredibly sweet. He was acting like her grandfather was a serial killer. Much the same way Deputy March had behaved when her last name came into play. "Same difference."

"It's not, and you well know it." Jolene limped her way over to Penelope and put her hand on her arm. "I don't think you tried to kill Hugh, though I wouldn't have blamed you. The boy often speaks before he thinks, is so alpha it can make your eyes roll, and pretty much thinks he's God's gift to women. You know what? You should get in the car and hit him again. Might knock some sense into him."

"Jolene?" asked Hugh, sounding flabbergasted.

"What?" questioned Jolene, a hand finding her hip. "You're acting like a fool, Lupine. Boy, I've known you since you were in diapers, running around with my nephew and Curt, getting into trouble. Trust me when I say, you need to be hit by a bus to get something through your thick head."

Hugh ran a hand through his shoulder-length dark brown hair. His dark brown gaze found Penelope and a tic started in his jaw. "She's a Messing."

"And you're a Lupine. So what," snapped Jolene, glancing around at the crowd that had started to gather.

A man who was just shy of six and a half feet tall stepped out into the street, blowing his nose before sneezing. He wore a pair of dress slacks and a pullover shirt. He looked to be around the age of thirty and while he was muscular, he was also lean. He wore a pair of black framed glasses that added to his appeal. There was a certain nerdy handsomeness to him that anyone looking at him would be able to see. Not to mention, he had a great smile.

"Aunt Jolene, what are you in the middle of now?" asked the man.

"Sigmund, I thought I told you to stay home and rest until your, um, allergies lightened up," said Jolene, glancing at Deputy March. She fidgeted with the front of her overalls and then positioned herself in a way that put her between the deputy and her nephew. It made Penelope instantly think of an overprotective momma bear looking out for her cub. While Sigmund did seem slightly nerdy (in the cutest way possible), he looked as if he could more than handle himself.

"Sig," Deputy March said, nodding his head at the man. "Can you please talk some sense into your aunt?"

Sigmund laughed. "I wish. She's as stubborn as a mule."

"Am not," stammered Jolene. She clenched her jaw and helped to prove her nephew's point.

Deputy March sighed. "This is going to be a long day. I regret that I didn't call in sick."

"Hi, Sig," said Buster. He shook a jar. "We're almost to a thousand now from Hugh alone. We'll have that new school built before you know it."

Sigmund withdrew an inhaler from his front pocket, brought it to his lips, and took two puffs before blowing his nose again. His eyes were glassy, and his nose was red. He looked miserable, yet still kept a smile on his face and somehow managed to be sexy through it all. "Go easy on him, Buster. He's operating without his training wheels today."

"I will hurt you," said Hugh with a snort that said he didn't mean it.

Sigmund smiled at her. "And who might you be?"

"She tried to kill Hugh," said Deputy March.

"I did not!" protested Penelope. The urge to run came over her, but she held her ground. She would not let them accuse her of anything else. She was a good person. She didn't kill people or intentionally run them over.

Sigmund's gaze found Hugh. "I'm surprised it took a woman this long to try to kill you. Honestly, I'd have figured one would have offed you years ago."

The lighter tone made Penelope calm slightly. And the longer she knew Hugh, the more she realized Sigmund probably wasn't kidding. Hugh had a way about him that certainly did wear on one's nerves, and bring out the urge to wring his neck. She was struggling with the impulse herself.

"You're a crap best friend," said Hugh.

"Lucky for you, you have two of us," reminded Sigmund. "Speaking of which, I'm off to meet Curt for morning coffee. Want to come?"

"He can't," said Jolene. "He's clearing up this mess he made. Tell the nice deputy that Penelope didn't try to kill you. She's already suspect number one in the double homicide that happened this morning." Her eyes darted to her nephew briefly.

Hugh grunted and took a giant step back from Penelope.

Sigmund laughed at Hugh. "You generally save this behavior for Wilber."

"That is her grandfather," said Deputy March as if that summed up everything perfectly.

Hugh tossed his hands in the air. "I cannot believe I thought Old Man Wil's granddaughter was hot. I was going to ask her out on a date. I sure know how to pick 'em. She's a murderer in a puppy dog sweater. Bet that throws suspicion off her."

Penelope squared her shoulders, taking extreme offense. "I didn't kill anyone, and I'll thank you kindly to check that tone with me. I don't know what you have against my grandfather, and I really don't care. Stop acting like what happened here was my fault. If you were crossing at a crosswalk or, I don't know, looking where you were walking, I wouldn't have clipped you with my car." She leveled her gaze on him. "And for the record, I'd have said no to going on a date with you. I like my men able to look both ways before crossing. How about we try this all over again. Only this time, I'm not going to be inclined to brake. I might just run right over you and back up for good measure."

Jolene and several other spectators laughed loudly. Sigmund tried to hide his amusement behind taking another puff of his inhaler. Buster held the jar out toward Hugh as if he was expecting something to happen, and Deputy March took a small step back from her.

They'd gathered quite a crowd of tourists. Several snapped photos of it all while others held their phones up, recording the events. She'd be an internet sensation by the end of the day. The girl who couldn't drive and who murdered people near cliffs for sport.

As she stood there, the subject of so many people's stares, she began to tear up. She'd only wanted to get away from Craig. Away from the city.

Her gaze moved to Hugh and she saw something flash in his eyes. Was it regret? She wasn't sure and she didn't care. He'd thrown her under the bus the moment he'd learned her last name.

Jerk.

Hugh sighed and then swallowed hard. "I'm sorry."

Jolene tapped her ear, making a big production out of it all. "Did I hear that right? Did Hugh apologize to someone?"

Buster's bottom lip poked out as he shook his head no. "Never thought I'd hear the day."

Sigmund grinned.

Hugh locked gazes with her. "I am sorry. I shouldn't have said what I did."

Penelope pointed at Hugh. "You had better tell Deputy March the truth and this time make sure he believes you."

Hugh groaned. "Fine. I walked out in front of her. She couldn't have stopped. It *was* my fault."

Deputy March glanced fleetingly at her before heading back to his SUV. He pulled away, never saying a word more on the matter. Somehow, she doubted she'd seen the last of him. She also wondered if something was in Everlasting's drinking water that produced such good-looking men who had such questionable personalities.

Jolene put her hand out and began to shoo onlookers. "Okay, folks, nothing more to see here. You've gotten your bit of excitement for the day. Be on your way."

Sigmund stayed in place. "Hugh, if you're going to ask her out, I'd do it fast. If you wait any longer, you'll do something else stupid and ruin your chances."

Hugh licked his lower lip. "She's Wilber's grand-daughter. He's never going to allow her to be around me. Not with the history our families have together."

Penelope watched him. "My grandfather doesn't run my life. And if you're asking, the answer is still no."

Hugh's jaw snapped shut as indignation shone on his attractive face.

Jolene laughed and clapped her hands. "I love it. I don't think any woman has ever told him no."

"Really? I pretty much want to chant it," said Penelope, crossing her arms over her chest. "No. No. No, and no."

Hugh's lips twitched. "You're even more beautiful standing there mad at me, wearing that ridiculous sweater, glaring at me. If I let you hit me again with your car, will you take pity on me and forgive me for letting stupid fall out of my mouth?"

Sigmund shook his head. "You're hopeless, Hugh."

Penelope entertained giving in, but having been burned by romance already, she wasn't ready to hop back into the frying pan. She exhaled and held her hand out to Hugh. "Penelope Messing. Nice to meet you, Hugh."

He paused before taking her hand. "Are we starting over?"

"We are," she said.

"This means you're going to let me take you out to eat?" he asked, sounding hopeful.

She pursed her lips. "I'd more than likely poison you."

His lips twitched before he gave her a full-on, big white smile. "Guess I'd have it coming. Plus, it would make your grandfather happy. And if I can survive Polly's cake, I can live through anything. It's a date then for dinner?"

She even smiled at that. "As much I want to say yes, I can't."

Sigmund and Buster snorted.

Hugh's cheeks reddened. "I'll write in the sky that you didn't hit me on purpose and that I'm a jerk. You don't need to keep trying to prove your point. Message received. Loud and clear."

"Say yes so we can see him actually write it in the sky," said Buster before backing up quickly from Hugh's reach.

Penelope spotted again what was written on the front of the man's jar and paused. "Why does that have Hugh's name on it?"

Buster grinned. "Because he bet Curt Warrick that he could make it a month without cursing and every time he messes up, he has to pay a fine. The money goes toward the middle school fund," said the man with pride. "We've made almost a grand off Hugh in only four days."

Hugh growled, and Penelope found herself stepping in front of Buster in a protective manner. "From what I heard him string together earlier, I'm shocked you've not made more."

"Me too," said Buster.

Sigmund laughed. "Hugh has the worst mouth. By the way, Hugh, Polly is looking for you."

Hugh's face scrunched. "She's going to try to force me to eat more cranberry cookies, isn't she?"

Sigmund grinned. "More than likely. You know how she likes to feed you. Plus, she still feels bad after the last incident. The one with the fleas."

"I hate cranberries," grumbled Hugh, and then he scratched at his leg. "And her baking terrifies me. I'm itching thinking about it."

Sigmund displayed a knowing grin. "Yeah, you should invest in a flea collar, just in case."

The people of Everlasting were odd. Very, very odd.

"Seriously though, I cannot eat anything with cranberries in it," stressed Hugh to Sigmund. "I really hate them."

Penelope glanced toward the huge banner strung across the street, announcing the Cranberry Festival. It looked to be a month of activities and eating, all celebrating the cranberry harvest. She snickered. He was in the wrong town if he hated cranberries. "You hate the very thing Everlasting is about to spend a month celebrating?"

He nodded. "Yes."

"Why am I not surprised?" she asked. "You seem the type to go against the grain whenever possible."

Sigmund snorted. "Look at that, she already knows you well."

Hugh stepped closer to her. "So, about dinner?"

Her hand went to her hip as she stared at him. With the way he'd behaved she wanted to make him work for a date with her, though she still harbored guilt over hitting him with her car. "What about it?"

He cleared his throat, drawing more laughs from his friends. They apparently reveled in seeing him on the spot. She had to admit that she did too.

"Um, will you do me the honor of having dinner with me?"

She touched her lower lip, considering his offer. He was everything Jolene had said he was, rough edges and all. But he was certainly sexy. That helped a lot. And she needed to take her mind off Craig. Maybe Hugh was just what she needed.

"Hey, I can also ask around about the bodies. I know everyone in town. Someone might know something." Hugh offered a sincere look, leading her to believe he wasn't toying with her. And she could use some help trying to clear her name, since Deputy March seemed to be looking no further than the end of his nose for another suspect.

She wanted to know more as well. After all, it was her backside that was on the line. "Can I come with you? I think I'm suspect number one in Deputy March's mind. I'd like to find out what happened for no other reason than to keep from spending the rest of my life wearing an orange jumpsuit."

He flashed another wicked grin. "I bet you'd look stunning in a jumpsuit."

She stared at him.

He put his hands up and laughed. "Hey, you make fire hydrant leggings look hot. A jumpsuit would be nothing for you to pull off. But seriously, I can take you around, and we can try to find out more about what happened with the bodies. And then we can eat. Sleuthing is bound to take it out of us."

He was right. They really would work up an appetite if they were hunting for clues on what had happened to the men. "Okay, but I reserve the right to poison you," she said succinctly.

He flashed a bad-boy smile. "I'd expect nothing less."

Buster eased closer to him.

Hugh glared at the small man. "You're not following me around with the damn jar all day."

Buster held it out. "That will be two dollars."

Sigmund smiled. "This is going to be an interesting month."

Chapter Seven

Hugh watched as Penelope drove off in her tiny rental car. Absently, he rubbed his leg, his gaze still locked on her as he stood off to the side of the street. He didn't want to admit the car had done more damage than he'd let on. It was embarrassing enough that he'd gotten hit by a car—a hybrid one at that. He didn't need to add insult to injury.

Sigmund remained, as did Buster, though Buster wisely put some space between them. Smart man. Hugh was just about to the breaking point with him. If Buster continued trailing him for the rest of the month, Hugh couldn't be held responsible for his actions, or for where they'd be dislodging the fine jar from Buster's body.

He didn't voice as much, but rather glanced off in the direction Penelope had gone. Only he would manage to walk out in front of someone as smoking hot as her, get hit by her car, and then find out she came from a long line of supernatural hunters. He'd known he should have simply let her be and thanked his lucky stars that she'd only caused him slight injury with the vehicle. Messings were a dangerous lot and weren't to be taken lightly.

Still, Hugh couldn't stop thinking about her. From her smell to her royal-blue eyes, everything about her had appealed to him on a base level. He even considered running after her car, just to be around her more.

You're pathetic.

He groaned at himself for his actions. This wasn't him. He didn't chase after women—okay, he had long ago when the neighbor girl moved away, but that didn't count.

Did it?

"Someone want to tell me how a Messing can look that good?" Hugh asked. "And why it is I asked her out on a date?"

Sigmund blew his nose before answering. "I'm shocked you're setting aside your hate of the family to even notice how attractive she is. And I've no idea what possessed you to ask her out. Though if you wouldn't have, I might have. She's stunning and seems very nice."

"For a Messing," said Hugh. His wolf's hackles raised slightly at the idea of Sigmund making a play for Penelope. He'd never had issue before with the idea of one of his friends asking a girl he found attractive out on a date. Why now? And why her?

"For anyone," countered Sigmund, ever the voice of reason. Out of his best friends, Sigmund was always the one who disliked violence and conflict. He was also the one who had talked the three of them out of more trouble than Hugh could even count while they were growing up. Sigmund had always had a way with words and an ability to smooth over just about anything.

"I like this new side of you," said Sigmund. "Maybe Penelope was just what you needed to come crashing into your life."

With a snort, Hugh nodded. "Literally."

He put his hands into his front pockets and glanced back in the direction of Wilber's shop. The hair on the back of his neck rose, and he shuddered. Was he insane? Asking out the granddaughter of a hunter was nuts. He'd been unable to help himself when he'd asked her out on a date. His wolf didn't seem to care that she came from a long line of supernatural murderers. It just wanted her.

Truth be told, he wanted her too.

She was strikingly beautiful and sassy. Not to mention quirky. The type of woman who marched to her own beat, unconcerned with fads and trends. That was appealing to him. A half grin spread over his face as he thought about her clothing. Not many could pull off making a puppy dog sweater sexy.

Penelope had. And there had been a certain vulner-ability in her eyes that made him want to wrap his arms around her and protect her from the world.

She was a Messing and could no doubt take care of herself. Heck, she could probably kill a man with nothing more than her pinky finger. Still, the alpha side of him wanted to keep her safe. To mark her as his.

Mine?

He jerked back, and a line of curses fell free of him.

Buster was there, jar in hand, smiling wide. "Pay up."

"Write a fat check for the month, Hugh," said Sigmund. "Or admit defeat and let Curt claim victory."

"Over my dead body," snapped Hugh.

Sigmund chuckled. "Hey, you're having dinner with a Messing. We might very well find your dead body later. Does that mean Curt wins by default? Also, it would bring Everlasting's daily total to three. A new record."

"You're a crap best friend," reminded Hugh. He didn't mean it. He, Curt, and Sigmund had been close since they were children. They'd always been there for one another, and while they were competi-tive, they were close.

Sigmund sneezed and then walked off, laughing more. "And you're going on a date with a hunter.

Get your last will and testament together. Any final words?"

Hugh shared his thoughts and Buster held the jar out.

"Twenty bucks for that." Buster stared after Sigmund. "His allergies are worse than normal this time of year. I don't think his new meds are helping. If anything, he seems worse. I feel bad for him. Being allergic to cranberries has to be hard."

"Yeah, I just hate them. They can't kill me like they can Sig."

"Look at you, seeing the bright side," said Buster, sounding way too chipper for Hugh's liking. "Next thing we know you'll be bursting into song."

Hugh grunted and walked in the direction of the marina. "I'll show you my bright side."

Buster gulped loudly behind him. "Tell me all about it in detail. The middle school needs more donations."

"You're about to be added to the day's body count," returned Hugh, only partially joking. "They tell me we're already at two. Want to make it three?"

Chapter Eight

Penelope couldn't hide her excitement as she stood just outside her grandfather's antiques shop. Twenty years had done nothing to take away from its charm and appeal. It looked exactly as she'd remembered it. There was still a small newspaper machine out front, with a shiny red candy machine standing next to it, filled to the brim with colorful gumballs. A black welcome mat was in front of large green wooden doors with glass panels. Operating hours were hand-painted on the glass panes. The brass knobs of the doors were still polished to perfection. Her grandfather had always had an eye for details and took preserving history very seriously.

"We are the caretakers of the past, present, and future," he used to say as he allowed her to help dust select items in the store. She'd loved every minute she'd been permitted to be his helper. She especially loved hearing the stories about the items in the shop, in what he had deemed the not-for-sale section.

Penelope caught sight of a man who looked to be in his late fifties or early sixties but was in actuality just over seventy. He had on a tan V-neck sweater with a striped collared shirt under it and a pair of dark brown dress slacks. His unruly salt-and-pepper hair hung to his ears, and the man's cheeks were rosy. He was a sight for sore eyes.

He'd never been a fan of Craig and would more than likely be happy they were no longer a couple. He'd also refrain from telling her that he'd told her so. That wasn't his style. He glanced up, his blue gaze finding hers. There was no mistaking the joy on his face. Relief swept through her.

He held an old camera in one hand and a green cloth in the other. There was no surprise in his eyes. If anything, he looked as if he'd been expecting her. The edges of his mouth curved upward, and he set the camera and the cloth down on the counter. He put his arms out wide and moved around the counter with a speed that impressed her.

Unable to stop herself, Penelope hurried into the shop and rushed to her grandfather, giving him a big hug. She squeezed him tight. "Grandpa!"

"Thought I might be seeing you," he said, his accent indicative of the region.

She drew back and eyed him. "You knew I'd come?"

He winked. "Yep."

Penelope pursed her lips. "I'm almost afraid to ask how. Remember that time you told me some lady who runs a bakery told you about a premonition she had?"

"Oh, Polly? She gets those a lot."

Penelope couldn't wait to meet Polly. Her name certainly came up a lot in conversation.

"Did she tell you I was coming to town?" she asked, not believing for a moment that any woman could see the future.

"Nope." He picked up the camera he'd been dusting and continued. The camera had embossed leather wrapped around the back and a brass mounting plate.

The geeky side of Penelope that lived for antiques sparked. She smiled wide. "Who is the manufacturer? I don't recognize the stamp. Is it mid-1800s?"

Her grandfather offered a sweet smile. "It is, but it's not made by anyone you'd know or have heard of. Sort of one of a kind." He winked as if he knew something more about the camera than he was letting on.

"What are you asking for it?" she inquired, ever the curious one. It was hard to shut off the auctioneer side of her personality.

He set it back in the cabinet gently. "To the right person, it's priceless. It can also be temperamental, and something one has to be sure doesn't lead them down a dark path."

"You know, you're even odder than me," she said, kissing his cheek quickly.

He hugged her again and then drew her back at arm's length, shaking his head in a disapproving manner. "They don't feed you enough in Chicago. Weren't you the one going on and on about the deep-dish pizzas there? Doesn't look like you eat them much."

She laughed then stepped back to take a look around the shop. "It hasn't changed at all. Neither have you."

He patted his nonexistent gut. "I'm old."

"Pfft. Hardly," she said before hugging him once more.

"How long are you in town for?" he asked, staying close to her. "Tell me for good. I'd love it if you lived here full time."

"I was planning on a week if that's all right with you."

"That isn't long enough. Call your boss and tell him you quit."

Penelope laughed once more. "Right. And do what to make a living then?"

He glanced around the shop, lifting a brow as he did. "Take over for me, of course. It's in your blood, you know. You'd make a wonderful keeper of the artifacts."

She sighed. He'd mentioned more than once wanting her to take over his shop. And while antiques were her life, she wasn't sure she could simply uproot all she knew and move to the tiny town of Everlasting. She liked her twenty-four-hour stores and access to great lattes a little too much to admit out loud. She had yet to see a coffee shop in town. "Do they have any chain coffee shops here?"

Her grandfather snorted in indignation. "No. We've got a few places that serve coffee. Polly's place, called Witch's Brew, makes a great cup of coffee. What would we need with any big-city chain? Besides, we're a little more than they could handle."

"Because the town is full of witches, werewolves, and magic?" she asked, a teasing note in her voice, the stories of her childhood filling her head. Her grandfather had been full of fantastical tales.

He grinned. "Exactly."

"Well, I've yet to meet a werewolf, or anything else remotely cool like that."

He laughed. "Not true. When you were little, you played with a werewolf nearly daily. He lived next door to you and your parents. He was such a sweet young boy. Turned into a foul-mouthed heathen."

She thought about the man she'd hit with her

rental car and the string of obscenities he'd managed to put together. "Does this supposed were-wolf still live around these parts?"

"Yep. Owns a fishing charter service down near the marina," said Grandpa Wil.

She thought about the man's t-shirt and the logo that had been on it. It had said something about a fishing charter. She paled. "He wouldn't, by chance, be named Hugh, would he?"

Her grandfather beamed. "Oh, you remember him? I can't say I'm thrilled he's who you remember from your time here, but at least it's a start."

"He sort of makes an impression," she blurted, recalling how incredibly handsome the man had been, even flat on his back, saying things unfit for most ears. She also recalled how much he'd seemed to loathe her family.

Her grandfather groaned. "Penelope, pick anyone but him. Have you met Curt Warrick yet? Now there is a good-looking young man who has a level head on his shoulders. He's not driven by testosterone."

"So you're saying Hugh reminds you of a wolf because he's manly?" she asked with a snort.

"That, and his kind are prone to fleas." Her grandfather headed toward the back of the shop, and she followed close behind him. He made his way to the door that separated the house from the store and entered, holding it open for her. They walked into an oversized kitchen. In the center of it was a round table. On it was a teapot, two cups on saucers, and a small plate of mini-sandwiches.

"Are you expecting someone?" she asked, wondering if, perhaps, he was dating.

He glanced over his shoulder at her. "I was expecting you."

She paused, positive he was only teasing her. He couldn't have known she was coming, could he? As she thought harder on it, she grinned. "Jolene called you and gave you a heads-up, didn't she?"

He drew to a stop at the mention of Jolene. "You met Jolene?"

"I did. She helped me find the town when I got all turned around out near a lighthouse during the storms."

He nodded, worrying his chin. "Cornelius was probably up to his old tricks again."

"Who?"

"Never mind," he said, taking a seat and pouring the tea. "How was Jolene? Did she look healthy?"

"She twisted her ankle and was limping, but other than that she seemed well," responded Penelope, unsure why her grandfather was acting so strangely. "She mentioned stopping by later to be sure I was all settled in at the bed-and-breakfast. I could tell her you asked about her."

He stiffened. "No. That's fine. And wait, what is

this nonsense about you staying at the B&B? You'll be staying here, with me. There is plenty of room. I already have your room all set up for you."

She took a seat across from him and added a lump of sugar to her tea. "And how was it you knew I'd be coming?"

"The crystal balls in my inventory told me," he said, no hint of a joke in his voice.

She laughed all the same. "Sure, Grandpa. Sure. Are those near the cursed tiki idols?"

"No. I keep the cursed idols in the basement. They tend to cause trouble if I don't." He sipped his tea.

She laughed, enjoying his active imagination. "Let me guess, they totally disappear and reappear all over the shop?"

"How did you guess?" he asked, looking impressed.

She snorted. "Your storytelling always lightens my mood."

He continued to sip his tea. "The crystal balls were vague on the details, but they told me you'd be coming."

"Did they tell you why?" she asked, her thoughts drifting back to Craig.

He nodded. "They said you'd come to find your mate and settle down. I'm not sure how that whiny brat you call a boyfriend is going to take the news that you'll be meeting your future husband, and frankly, I don't much care."

There was so much she wanted to say to his comment, but she didn't know where to start. "Grandpa, Craig dumped me. He's engaged to someone else now."

"Want me to break his legs?" he asked, no note of teasing in his voice.

Her eyes widened. "Grandpa!"

"What? I didn't offer to kill him. But I could. Just let me know. I can be there and back in the blink of an eye. I have a great piece I picked up in England years ago that lets me teleport."

She laughed, assuming he was joking. "You know, talk like that is probably why Deputy March is sure I'm up to no good."

Her grandfather touched the table lightly. "You've talked with Deputy March?"

"Yes, he questioned me about two men found dead near the cliffs. He says they suspect foul play and that they're still trying to identify the men. I guess I was the last person seen in the area before they were found dead."

He stood quickly. "I'll be right back. Watch the shop for me."

"Grandpa?"

He glanced at her. "If any FOLs come in, show them the door with your foot."

"FOLs?" she asked, lost as to what was happening.

"Fraternal Order of Light members," he said, as if she should know what that means. "They're always trying to get their hands on my artifacts."

She opened her mouth to question it all, but her grandfather continued. "And should someone from the Collective try to come in, the place is warded. Ignore the big boom and the shaking. Happens each time."

With that, he hurried out the back door, leaving Penelope sitting there completely dumbfounded. Fraternal Order of Light? Collective? What rabbit hole had she fallen down?

Chapter Nine

Penelope busied herself with dusting items in a cabinet that was clearly labeled not for sale as customers looked at the various antiques available in the shop. The shop itself was much larger than it appeared from the street. It had an upper level and an enormous basement, all stuffed to the brim with antiques and artifacts. If her grandfather ever let her have an auction with the items, she could make him a fortune, but that wasn't his style.

She knew he did well for himself as noted in the ledgers on the back-office desk, but he lived modestly. She had a lot in common with him. Their shared love of antiques and living below their means.

"I saw them first," a blonde woman said, grabbing hold of an elephant figurine. Her blonde hair was pulled back so tightly from her face that it pulled at her features, making them look sharp. She held the figure close as another woman, a redhead, gently lifted its twin.

"Actually, I was here looking at them for the last ten minutes," said the redhead, her voice soft. Penelope knew the woman was telling the truth. She'd seen the woman there, admiring the figurines, evidently debating on getting them.

Penelope glanced at the figurines and sighed. No wonder the women wanted them. Her grandfather had scored a matched pair of Chinese famille rose porcelain figures that looked like they might double as candlestick holders. She moved out from behind the counter and approached the women with caution. The blonde especially looked as if she were ready to pounce.

The woman to the left, with big, bright red curls, looked at Penelope. "I swear that I saw these first. I was trying to decide if I should buy them or not. Then she came along and well…"

The blonde huffed and lifted her chin. "I want them. I'll pay double."

Penelope held out her hand to the redhead, sensing she'd have a better shot at getting the figure from her rather than the blonde. "If I may."

Reluctantly, the redhead handed over the elephant.

Penelope ran her fingers over the smooth item, impressed with the detail that remained upon it.

The colors were still bright. The elephant had a small vase upon its back, painted. The attention to detail was impressive. There wasn't a chip or fracture on it, a testament to the care that had been taken with it over its long life. A smile touched Penelope's lips as she realized the item was from the Qing Dynasty. She looked at the blonde. "Double? Are you sure?"

The woman's look never faltered. "I know what they're worth and yes, I'll pay double."

The redhead frowned. "How much is double?"

When Penelope told her the price, which was enough to buy a small car, the redhead appeared sad. She reached out, lovingly stroking the figure Penelope held, and then lifted it from her.

When the blonde tried to snatch hold of it, showing no regard for the item, Penelope's temper flared.

She caught hold of it and gave the blonde a look that backed her up. She also took the other candlestick holder from the woman. "Thank you for the offer, but the price marked is the price. And I believe this woman was here first."

The blonde snapped back and then glared at Penelope. "Why I've never."

"Really, with your winning disposition I'd have guessed you run into this a lot," returned Penelope, offering a hundred-watt smile.

With that, the blonde stormed away, her

tantrum lessened by the light ding of the bell above the door to the shop. Dinging never really added anything to a dramatic exit.

The redheaded woman teared up. "I love them, but the price is just too steep for me."

The strangest urge to offer a discount came over her, and she wasn't sure she should. She knew what the figures would go for at auction and they were priced under that. Far under it. "I'm sorry, but my grandfather owns the shop, and I don't feel comfortable changing his pre-marked prices."

The phone to the shop rang three times before an answering machine picked up. The message played of her grandfather sounding lost as to how to properly work the machine while he recorded a message. There was a beep, and her grandfather's voice came over the room. "Penelope, sorry I had to rush off. I'm a bit tied up now so feel free to handle the shop any way you see fit. Don't forget to take a lunch hour too. Oh, and can you mark down the Chinese famille rose porcelain elephant figures? Discount them down by twenty percent. I'm sure they'll find the right home then." He hung up.

Penelope stood there a moment, holding the figures, feeling a bit like she'd entered the Twilight Zone. She glanced at the redheaded woman. "Turns out I can offer a twenty percent discount on them."

"Sold!" the woman shouted, smiling wide a second before tears came to her eyes. "My mother used to collect these types of things, and when I saw them, they made me think of her. I lost her a year ago today."

Penelope paused. "I'm sorry."

"Thank you so much," said the woman, following Penelope to the register.

Within a few short minutes, Penelope had the figures wrapped securely and bagged and was running the woman's credit card. She handed the woman her receipt and waved as the woman hurried away.

The steady stream of patrons died down, and Penelope decided it was the perfect time to take a lunch break. She closed up the shop and headed out front. She turned the sign around in the window, letting it read *out to lunch* as she locked the shop door.

At first she'd been concerned about running the shop without Grandpa there. It wasn't as if she had experience running a store. Tourists had filtered in and out all morning, asking questions about various pieces. With her background with antiques and auctions, answering their inquiries was easy. As much as she hated to admit it, she liked working in the shop more than at the auction house.

Her stomach grumbled, reminding her that she was hungry. She double-checked the sign letting patrons know that she'd be out to lunch was showing. She then turned to survey downtown Everlasting, looking for a spot to eat. A fairly long line was out the door of Chickadee's Diner, so she headed across the street toward it.

She took her spot at the end of the line, behind a tall, well-built, and well-dressed gentleman. His dark hair hung just past his ears and was swept back from his handsome face. As he turned, his green gaze locked on her. His brow rose. "Interesting outfit."

She smiled. "Thanks."

From the looks of his designer suit, he wouldn't be caught dead in a puppy dog sweater.

He grinned. "Big fan of dogs?"

"I love them," she said before sneezing rapidly.

His smile widened. "Bless you."

She sneezed again. Embarrassed, she blushed. "Sorry. I usually only sneeze around cats."

His eyes widened a second before he cleared his throat, tugging at his collar. "That *is* strange."

"Totally," she said, glancing at the long line. "The food here must be awesome."

"It is," he said with a look that could charm just about any woman. "You're new to town. I haven't seen you here before."

"I'm just visiting. I'm here to see my grandfather for a week or so and then it's back to Chicago for me."

He watched her. "I see. A Windy City girl? I

could have sworn you have hints of a Southern accent when you talk."

"I was actually born here but moved to Mississippi at a young age. Went to college in Chicago and then stayed there to work."

"Ah, that explains the accent." He stepped forward as the line moved up a little. "Who is your grandfather?"

"I'm not sure I should tell you."

He faced her more. "Why? Don't trust me? I could gather character references if you'd like. Most everyone around here knows me."

"I don't even know your name," she said.

He held out a well-manicured hand. "Curt Warrick."

"The same Curt who made a bet with Hugh?" she asked, remembering the back and forth between Hugh and Sigmund.

Curt appeared impressed. "One and the same. Dare I ask how you know about the bet?"

"I got a firsthand look at the fining system," she mused. "After I hit Hugh with my car."

Curt tossed his head back and laughed loudly, drawing the attention of the others waiting in line. "Tell me he required medical attention."

She gasped. "No. And aren't you his friend?"

"I am."

"Then why would you want him to get hurt?"

Curt waved a hand in the air. "Oh, have no fear.

Hugh has a *really* hard head. He'd be fine. And he heals fast. We both do."

"You're kind of weird," she blurted.

"I'm not the one wearing a puppy dog and fire hydrants," he said with a wink.

"Fair point."

Chapter Ten

Hugh steadied Petey as the old man stumbled slightly leaving the Magic Eight Ball. Thankfully, Hugh had managed to shake Buster for a while. He'd last seen Buster racing in the direction of the coffee shop, looking frantic.

Perfect.

Hugh sighed. As predicted, he'd found Petey at the bar, out cold, face first on a table.

Oddly enough, a plate of Polly's famous cranberry cookies had been next to the man. With Polly, one never knew what might be tainted with magic, so Hugh threw the cookies away. Once, he'd foolishly eaten a piece of cake she'd made him, and he'd gotten stuck in wolf form for an entire week. As if that wasn't bad enough, he'd gotten fleas that week as well. Petey had been left having to give Hugh a flea dip, all the while doing his best to keep from laughing at the situation. Turns out, she'd been testing a potion and wanted to see the side effects on a shifter. Hugh had been the only shifter dumb enough to eat the cake.

From what Hugh had heard, Polly's niece Anna no longer permitted Polly in the kitchen at the bakery, but Hugh knew what a sly fox the old woman was, and didn't trust she wouldn't try something else. She'd been at him for days to clean up his mouth and win the bet against Curt. While it was great to have her help, it also worried him. Polly was always well meaning, but her assistance and support often came with a level of unpredictable chaos.

Petey wore bright yellow rain gear in the form of bib suspenders and a jacket with a detachable hood. The color was so bright it bordered on obnoxious. Paired with fishing boots, a flannel shirt, and a knit cap, Petey looked a lot like Quint from the movie *Jaws*. The two sounded a great deal alike as well. If Hugh didn't know better, he'd have sworn the actor had based his portrayal of the character on Petey.

Petey was an old-school fisherman who didn't care about trends or what was acceptable or not. The man had served in the navy, and sometimes his mind remained there, stuck in the past, in battles long ago. Hugh was always patient with him, understanding the man had lived a hard life. As a fellow wolf-shifter, Hugh felt Petey was his responsibility. Pack took care of pack. Period.

Now Petey owned and operated the bait and tackle shop in town and helped do guided tours with Hugh's fishing charter. All normally went well until Petey decided it was time to tie on too many at the Magic Eight Ball. Hugh would call Shorty later and discuss cutting Petey off sooner.

The people of Everlasting didn't mind his outbursts or his oddities.

"What time is it? I gotta get my traps in," said Petey, falling slightly against the exterior of the Magic Eight Ball. "Lobsters are out there, wanting me to catch 'em."

Hugh sighed. "Petey, let's get you home so you can finish sleeping this off."

"It is what it is," said Petey, no longer making sense—not that he was well known for making a ton of sense to start with.

"Yep, now come on. You need to shower and rest. You smell like you took a bath in a bottle of whiskey."

"Been there. Done that. Don't want to waste good whiskey on it again."

Hugh groaned. "Petey, you have to stop this."

The old man drew up short and pointed at him. "I'll show you where a bear goes in the woods."

Hugh nearly laughed at the threat (if it could even be called as much). "Okay. Show me later. For now, come on, or I'm going to toss you over my shoulder and carry you."

Petey lifted his fists in a manner that said he was ready for a boxing match. "You're all bark and no bite. My wolf can kick your wolf's backside."

Hugh snorted. "And you're a walking book of idioms."

"Drastic times call for drastic measures," supplied Petey, slurring his words somewhat.

"Yeah. Sure they do. Let's go. Tourists are out and about now, and we don't need pictures of you all over the internet in that outfit. You look like that guy from the fish sticks box had a rough night."

"What's a fish stick?" asked Petey.

Hugh paused. "I'm not exactly sure. I probably don't want to know."

Petey stood as straight and steady as he could, considering the state he was in. Hugh ended up having to slide an arm under Petey's and lift him partially off the ground, doing his best to make it appear as if Petey was still in control.

"Whoa," breathed Petey, glancing down at his feet. "I'm floating."

Hugh said nothing as he headed back in the direction of the marina. Several locals walked past, each looking as if they understood Hugh's current plight. A group of tourists neared and one pointed to Petey.

"Look, honey," the woman said. "Everlasting has homeless people."

Hugh growled low in his throat, making the woman and her husband hurry along their way. Hugh looked ahead—and froze as he spotted Penelope in the line out in front of Chickadee's Diner. That didn't surprise him as the diner had great food. What *did* catch him off guard was who she was conversing with.

Curt.

The wolf in Hugh unfurled and tried to push upward. As much as Hugh attempted to keep hold of it, he failed and felt his upper arms suddenly covered in a light gray coating of fur.

Petey laughed. "Oops. Letting the wolf out of the bag, are you?"

Nervous, Hugh's gaze darted around as he turned into a small alley with Petey, hoping to avoid being seen by any tourists. He'd thought the threat of Buster losing control and turning into a were-rat was the worst thing he'd have to deal with today.

How wrong he'd been.

He opened his mouth to speak but found his incisors lengthening quickly as his jaw began to shift shapes. The sound of Penelope's laugh carried across the street and made his gut twist. Anger coursed through him, and he found himself wanting to seek out Curt and end the man for daring to not only be close to Penelope but make her laugh as well.

Mine.

The word raced through his head, causing additional panic to assail him. That did nothing to help him find his center and gain control of his shifter side. If anything, it made it worse. He released his hold on Petey and lurched back, staring down at his hands as claws emerged from his fingertips.

What was happening to him?

Petey pointed to his hands and laughed loudly. "That is a horse of a different color."

He shot the man a panic-stricken look.

Petey drew upon a resolve that Hugh wasn't aware the old man had. He touched Hugh's shoulder and gave it a good squeeze. "Calm yourself there, boy, else you'll be peeing on a fire hydrant soon."

That did it.

Hugh pulled on his control and managed to get his body to return to human form. His hands shook as he thought about how close to a full shift he'd come in broad daylight, out in the public's eye. Worse yet, he was thinking of a woman in terms of being his and his alone.

He was not a one-woman man.

He was a man who played the field and avoided commitments at all cost.

Why was he suddenly all about Penelope? A

woman who was a direct descendant of a family he loathed and feared?

"I'm broken," he said softly.

"Keep your chin up," said Petey, glancing behind him and then at Hugh. "Did you see where I left my catch?"

"What?" asked Hugh.

"I have a giant squid. It was wearing a wrist-watch. Caught it on Main Street last night," said Petey. "The darn thing walked right past me. Had the head of a squid, the legs of a man, and a whole lotta arms. It was headed in the direction of the lighthouse."

Hugh stared blankly at the man. Everlasting was known for weird and wacky occurrences, but a giant walking squid was pushing the boundaries. Next Petey would be talking about dancing elephants. "How much did you drink?"

"There you are," said Buster, coming around the corner, sweat dripping from his temples. "I've been looking everywhere for you."

Hugh groaned. Did the man have him LoJacked? How did he keep finding him, and didn't he have a life outside of following Hugh around?

Buster had the jar in one hand and a small cup of coffee in the other. He thrust the coffee at Hugh. "Here. I stopped by Witch's Brew, and Anna sent this coffee over for you."

"Anna did?" Hugh asked, making sure Polly had nothing to do with the coffee.

Buster nodded.

Hugh took the cup and was about to hand it to Petey to help sober him up when the overwhelming urge to drink it came over him. He downed it quickly.

Buster stepped back. "Well, Polly said that Anna wanted you to have it when she gave it to me."

Hugh's eyes bulged. "Polly gave it to you?"

Buster nodded once more. "Why?"

Hugh lunged at him only to be caught by Petey. "No killing the were-rat. There is paperwork, and you hate paperwork."

Growling, Hugh leveled a hard look on Buster. "If I get stuck in wolf form for a week again, I'm going to eat you."

Buster gulped.

Hugh decided to let his thoughts on the matter rip. "You son-of-a-biscuit, bacon-loving daisy-head."

Buster and Petey shared a look as Hugh shook his head, unsure why he'd said what he did. That certainly wasn't what he'd been aiming at. "What the ever-loving peanut butter and jelly sandwich did I just say?"

Ever-loving peanut butter?

Petey raised his hand. "Uh, I'm not sure what you just said there either. Am I still drunk? Anyone else happen to notice a giant walking squid? I swear I left him out here last night. Never met a squid that could untie knots, but he got out of my ties."

Buster paled and took a step back, his attention on Hugh.

Hugh glared at him. "I'm going to rip the tags off your mattresses."

What?

Rip the tags off mattresses?

Petey scratched his head. "I never thought I'd say this, but I think I drank too much. Hugh is talking like he's in preschool. Where is the foul-mouthed wolf-shifter we've all come to know and loathe?"

Buster licked his lower lip. "Erm, Polly mentioned something about the bet being a sure thing now."

Hugh thought about the coffee he'd downed, and knew then Polly had cooked up a potion. He just wasn't sure what all the side effects would be. One was clearly the inability to curse. He glared at Buster. "Fiddlesticks!"

Buster burst into laughter. Petey followed suit.

Hugh's ears reddened as he grabbed his wallet from his pocket and pulled out a ten to hand to Buster. "Here. We all know what I meant to say."

Buster kept laughing. "I can't take money for fiddlesticks. Wait until I tell Sigmund and Curt about this."

"Barnacles!" exclaimed Hugh, his anger in full force but his words sorely lacking.

Petey laughed more, bending and patting his knee for effect. "This is great."

Buster nodded in agreement. "No one will believe it until they hear it."

Petey stopped laughing and scratched his scruffy chin. His salt-and-pepper hair stuck out from under his knit cap in all directions. "Hugh may not be able to curse, but he probably could still eat you. So I'd be careful there, Buster."

Hugh perked at the idea.

Buster held the jar out to him. "Here. Consider it a refund."

Hugh caught the jar a second before Buster released it, leaving Hugh standing there with his curse jar and a slightly sober Petey. He glanced at Petey and then froze as the sound of Penelope's laughter found him once more.

The alpha side of him responded, leaving him no choice but to head out of the alley and back onto Main Street. She was like a siren, and he couldn't help but answer her call.

Was he right to first think she was dangerous? She was a Messing after all. Was she why he was suddenly broken?

Petey followed close behind. "Are we off to see a man about a horse, or a meddlesome witch about a potion?"

Hugh ignored him, focusing instead on Penelope. She was still in line with Curt, looking entirely too pleased with the man's company. The next thing Hugh knew, he was marching across the street, his sights set on the woman. If she thought she was going to fall for the charms of Curt, she was wrong. She was his woman. Not Curt's.

Mine?

He tripped over his own two feet in the middle of Main Street and nearly fell flat on his face. He recovered, rather ungracefully, and found all eyes on him.

Buster laughed so loud that Hugh considered turning around and body slamming the man. He resisted. It was hard.

Curt grinned and smoothed his jacket front down. "Hugh, I see you've taken to doing your own stunts now too. How is our bet coming? Willing to concede?"

"How about I shove my sunflower up your whoops-a-daisy?" As the ridiculous question left his lips, he remembered what Polly had done and cringed.

Penelope's expression lightened more. "Your what up his what?"

Hugh grunted.

Curt smiled wide, looking entirely too pleased with himself for Hugh's liking. "Dare I ask what is going on with you?"

"Eat your vegetables," snapped Hugh, meaning anything but that. His mouth and brain didn't want to connect.

Curt snorted. "This is an interesting change. Are you going to double dog dare me next?"

"Caramel fudge," returned Hugh, his anger growing, but he found he was unable to articulate it the way he used to. "Fiddlesticks."

Penelope beamed. "I like it. I'm going to have to use that one. My go-to is typically 'hold the pickles,' but I see room for improvement."

Wait. She liked this side of him?

Great.

She's not only beautiful, and from a family known to hunt mine, she's nuts too.

He found he didn't care. He still wanted her. More than wanted her, and he'd be damned if he let Curt get his hooks into her. Curt was more of a womanizer than Hugh, and that was saying something.

"Go away," he snapped at Curt.

"Rude, seeing as how I was here first," returned Curt, grinning.

Penelope launched into a fit of sneezes. "Excuse me. I think something in Everlasting doesn't agree with me. I swear I normally only sneeze this much around cats."

Hugh and Curt locked gazes. A slow, calculated smile spread over Hugh's face as he heard Penelope talk about being allergic to cats. "Does that apply to large-breed cats as well or just domesticated ones?"

Curt's eyes widened.

Penelope stepped closer to Hugh, and he nearly leaped with joy. "Big ones too. I always sneeze at the zoo when I'm around large cat breeds. Lions are the worst for me."

Hugh couldn't stop the laugh that bubbled up from him. Curt was a lion-shifter. Could it get any better than this? Maybe she'd have an allergy to piles of money too. That would totally rule out Curt.

Petey and Buster eased closer.

Petey offered Penelope a wide smile, despite the fact he smelled like he'd been distilling whiskey all night. "Do my eyes deceive me or has a mermaid come from the sea to wow us with her beauty?"

Penelope let him take her hand and seemed pleased when Petey kissed the back of it. "Why thank you."

Hugh simply stared at his longtime friend, wondering if he was possessed. Petey was never flowery. The most romantic thing he did was take Polly his catch of the day. And even that consisted of him wrapping a fish in newspapers and plunking it down on the woman's counter, giving her a smile that lacked all its teeth.

"Petey?" asked Buster. "Are you still drunk?"

"Hi again, Buster," said Penelope. "Why does Hugh have the fine jar now?"

"Conceding?" asked Curt, looking hopeful.

Hugh considered using hand gestures but refrained. "Eat a fish stick."

"What in tarnation is a fish stick?" demanded Petey.

Curt's amused expression drove Hugh mad. "Something you want to share with the group? Why are you suddenly insulting me as if you're three years old?"

"Told ya you sounded like a preschooler," said Petey.

"Figured when in Rome," said Hugh, narrowing his gaze on his longtime friend. If the man wasn't one of the closest people to Hugh, he'd consider killing him just because of how arrogant Curt tended to be.

The line moved forward and Betsy, a waitress at the diner, peeked out at them and smiled wide, chomping her gum as she did. "A table for five?"

"Yes," said Buster.

"No," answered Hugh and Curt.

Hugh reached out, snaked an arm around Penelope's waist, and dragged her against him. "A table for the two of us, please, Betsy."

"Oh really?" asked Curt.

Penelope pried Hugh's arm off her. "What are you doing? Only this morning, you were debating on telling Deputy March I ran you over on purpose."

"I apologized for that," said Hugh. "Besides, you're the one who hit me."

She snorted. "Because you haven't learned how to cross a street yet."

"Are we eating now or what?" asked Petey. "I'm starving."

Buster eased closer to Petey. "Betsy, Petey and I will sit at the counter."

"Fine by me," said Betsy, holding the door open for them. She then looked to Hugh, Curt, and Penelope. "What about you three?"

Penelope squared her shoulders. "Hugh and Curt are sitting together. I'll take a spot at the counter next to Petey and Buster please. Thank you."

Curt appeared amused by her antics. "It would appear the lady doesn't want anything to do with either of us."

"*The lady* is having dinner with me. She already agreed, and there are no take-backs."

"Yep, still sounding like a three-year-old," said Curt.

Penelope followed Betsy into the diner, leaving Hugh with Curt. "Kiss my grits."

"Uh, thanks, but no thanks," said Curt with a snort.

Chapter Eleven

Penelope turned the shop sign to read closed and was about to pull the shades when Hugh appeared at the door. He stood just outside, looking at it as if it might bite. He took a few steps back from the shop front and then glanced around before taking a deep breath and approaching the door once more. He spotted her and then seemed to relax.

The last she'd seen him had been when she'd waved to him from across the diner, enjoying seeing him stuck eating lunch with Curt. She'd had a wonderful lunch with Petey and Buster. Though Petey had smelled as if he'd bathed in whiskey. The older man could certainly eat. He'd polished off three full plates of the lunch special before she'd even made a dent in her bowl of soup. Buster had a healthy appetite too. She'd said her goodbyes and had headed back to the shop, leaving Hugh with his friend.

She opened the door and stood there. "We're closed."

"I know," he said. "It's why I'm here. You agreed to have dinner with me tonight, and since you didn't let me near you for lunch, I came to cash in."

She opened her mouth to protest.

He lifted a hand. "And I've found some information about the dead guys."

Her curiosity got the better of her, and she backed up, holding the door open for him. "Okay, you win. Come on in. I have to finish closing up the shop for the evening."

Hugh swallowed hard and tugged at his shirt collar. "Can't Wil do that? Is he here?"

She noticed Hugh had yet to put a foot over the threshold of the shop. "Grandpa ran out of here early this morning and has called a few times throughout the day. Looks like I'm on my own. I just have a few things to finish up first. Come on in."

He stilled. "Uh, I'm good here."

"You're not afraid to come in, are you?" She laughed. "I don't bite."

"If you did bite it would only turn me on more," he said before letting out a long, slow breath. "Fiddlesticks."

She laughed at his soft curse, and his face was

suddenly a wash of brilliant crimson. "Are you coming in or are you going to stand out there, leaving the impression that you're terrified of my grandfather's antiques store?"

He begrudgingly entered, extremely slowly, glancing around as if he were expecting the roof to cave in on him at any moment. "This is the first time I've ever been in here."

"Really? Why? Not a big fan of antiques?"

"Not a big fan of hunters," he said quickly.

"My grandfather doesn't hunt. He isn't a fan of killing animals either."

He snorted. "Is that what he told you?"

She didn't comment but rather went to the register to finish gathering the day's receipts to tally. Hugh followed close behind. So close that when she stopped to adjust a sign on a chair, telling people not to sit on it, Hugh slammed into her, knocking her forward.

She gasped.

He caught her around the waist and steadied her quickly, causing warmth to spread through her body. She gasped again. Did the man have to not only be incredibly good-looking but also have super-fast reflexes? She really was an accident waiting to happen and truly could use someone around her to keep her from walking off cliffs.

"Sorry," he said softly, easing his hands off her hips.

She twisted to face him, her intent to thank him. As she lifted her head to look him in the eyes, his lips met hers.

For a moment, Penelope's mind went totally and completely blank. Before she realized it, her palms were pressed to his steely chest as their tongues danced intimately with one another.

Coming to her senses, Penelope broke the kiss and stared up at Hugh.

His eyes were closed, and he looked as if he'd gotten as swept up in it all as she had. When he looked at her, there was hunger in his gaze. "Ready to go solve some murders and then get some dinner?"

A laugh bubbled up from her. "As soon as I finish up here. Are you going to be okay waiting in here?"

He stood there, his hands on her hips once again. "I find I'm liking this place more and more."

She smiled.

He looked at a shelving unit near her and lifted a brow. "What in the world is that?"

She followed his gaze to the shelf and found a case of eyes staring back at her. "Those are antique glass eyes."

He shuddered. "They give me the willies."

"Come on, a big strong guy like you is creeped out by old glass eyes?" she teased.

He took a step back. "Yes."

Laughing, she pointed to the other side of the shop. "There is a duchesse chair over there. You can wait there for me."

He took a step in that direction then paused. "Uh, there are like a hundred chairs in here. What in the world is a duchesse one?"

Penelope walked to the long chair that was near the wall and touched it. "This is a duchesse chair."

"You want me to sit on a fainting sofa?" he asked, shaking his head. Despite his protest, he sauntered over to the chair.

She suppressed a grin. "We've established you're delicate. You are scared of old glass eyes."

The edges of his mouth twitched before he laughed and sat. "Do your thing. I'll be here, being all delicate."

She wasn't sure the man could ever actually be thought of as delicate. Everything about him screamed alpha male. He oozed testosterone. He was the type of guy who looked like he could bench press a small house. Craig hadn't been like that. He'd been one of those men who was always worried about having a manicure and never having a hair out of place on his head. She couldn't imagine Hugh ever showing his face in a salon. He was rugged, and that was a huge turn-on.

Penelope hurried through the paperwork for the shop, happy that her grandfather had detailed notes on how to do it all. The man seemed to have detailed notes on just about everything in the shop. Even the price tags contained the price, the item's name, and a brief history. Some items had signs near them with additional handwritten information regarding what they were and where they were from. His attention to detail was impressive. And while Penelope had that same level of commitment to antiques and the auction house, it did not extend to her personal life or her apartment.

As she finished double-checking the daily logs against the instructions on how to do them, she paused. Had her grandfather written out how to do everything because he was getting ready to retire or sell the shop? Did he really need her there rather than in Chicago?

The more she looked around the shop, the more she could see herself there, day in and day out. But could she give up all she'd worked so hard for in Chicago?

As much as she loved her twenty-four-hour-a-day amenities in the Windy City, she found Everlasting was growing on her. And quickly too. In less than a day, she was already dreaming about the possibility of making it permanent. Did she dare?

She finished the day's paperwork and found Hugh asleep in the duchesse chair, snoring softly. His body was far too long for it, so his legs and feet hung off the end. He had one arm tossed up and partially over his head while the other arm was across his washboard abs. He looked like a fallen god there and as the sun poked in from a window high above, a ray of light found its way to his face. It illuminated him in a way that made her breath catch. She already knew he was incredibly handsome, but it looked like even Mother Nature was swept up with his good looks. He didn't so much as budge as the faint light continued to cover his face. She almost hated to wake him.

If he spent too much time resting there, he'd undoubtedly get a stiff neck, and she couldn't let that happen. Then she'd be compelled to offer to massage him, and that would lead to her touching his sinful body. Her willpower couldn't handle all that manliness, and she wasn't ready to go down the path that would lead to. At least not just yet.

She nudged his foot, and he shot out of the chair at a rate of speed that shocked her. She'd never seen anyone move that fast.

He glanced around wildly, looking as if he expected a frontal attack or perhaps an explosion. "What the blueberry pancakes?"

She stifled a laugh at his outburst. His colorful expressions made hers appear less odd, and she liked that. Liked knowing someone else got her, quirks and all. "You certainly have a way with words."

It took Hugh a few seconds to get his bearings

about him and then he calmed. "Yeah, I have Polly to thank for that."

"I have got to meet this woman," she returned, wanting to see the woman whose name had come up more than once since her arrival in Everlasting.

Hugh rubbed the back of his neck then stretched his arms high above his head, causing his shirt to pull up. As suspected, laundry could be done off his torso. Penelope nearly groaned as desire raced through her. Real men didn't come built that way. Was he really a fallen god? One who cursed using words like "fish sticks"?

Hugh's lips curved upward, his grin one that said come hither. "Yeah, with Polly, just don't eat or drink anything from her and you're fine."

"Oh, is she a bad cook?" asked Penelope.

"Nope. She's a great cook. The problem is, you always get more than you bargain for." He stretched again. "Once I got fleas."

She snorted. "What?"

He eased her hand into his and lifted it, planting a kiss on the back of it. "Never mind. Are you all set now?"

"I am. What did you find out about the men they discovered this morning?"

"They weren't locals," he said. "That is peculiar in itself. The spot they were found in isn't really easy to find unless you know the area well, and if the time of death lines up to what they think, that means these guys were out there at a time of night when no one, not even locals, go there."

"Do you think they came by way of boat?" she asked.

"No. The storms that blew through would have made that spot a bad place to take a boat. There is a great cove just down a bit that is well known and offers shelter from rough seas. Plus, there was no evidence of a boat wreck there or where the current tends to dump things from there. My guess is those men were down there on foot, and that takes some doing. The path to that area is hard to find even when you are from here. And really, anyone down there that time of the night, in those storms, has to have been up to no good."

"Does Deputy March have any leads yet? Other than me?"

Hugh shook his head. "No. He's still looking at you for this from what I can gather. He hasn't returned my calls yet today, and that is strange. Jake and I are friends. The last I saw of him was this morning after I walked in front of your car."

"Jake?" she questioned, unsure who they were talking about.

Hugh snorted. "You know him as Deputy March, but his name is Jake Majoy."

Penelope pursed her lips. "So why does he go by Deputy March?"

Laughing, Hugh stayed close to her. "That

would be the sheriff's doing. She's going through what we like to call a midlife crisis. Though none of us say that to her face. She's taken to hiring men of a certain age group, with certain physical traits. Anyways, someone made the suggestion a couple of years back to have the deputies pose for a calendar, with the proceeds going to charity. They did. The rest is history. I'm pretty sure the fire department is now considering doing the same thing. Those guys don't like all the attention the deputies are getting."

Penelope's face lit. "Aha, and Deputy March must have been shown for the month of March."

"You got it. All the guys are now known by their calendar month, not their names," said Hugh.

Penelope snorted. "I haven't met the sheriff, but I already like her."

Hugh kept hold of her hand as she led him through the shop and into her grandfather's house. When she entered the kitchen, she found a note on the table and her bags near the staircase. Confused as to how her luggage managed to find its way to her at her grandfather's, rather than the B&B address she'd given the airlines, she stepped forward.

Lifting the note, she read it out loud. "Sandra from the B&B rang to let me know your luggage arrived. I went ahead and picked up your things. You'll be staying with me, where you belong. I ran into Betsy from Chickadee's Diner, and she told me you enjoyed the bean soup, so I put more in the fridge if you need it. I'll be out late tonight, don't wait up. Love you, Grandpa."

Hugh tensed and released her hand. "I wonder what he's up to. Did he say why he was leaving this morning? Seems strange he'd take off when you only just got into town."

"He hightailed it out of here right after I told him Deputy March liked me for the double homicide." Penelope had to agree that it was odd her grandfather would spend her first full day in Everlasting away from her. But she'd dropped in on him unannounced, and he had a life of his own. It was to be expected that he couldn't stop everything at a moment's notice.

Hugh grabbed his cell from his back pocket and pressed a button. "Jake, it's me again. Call me back so I know that Wilber doesn't have you locked in a dungeon somewhere while he tortures you."

Penelope gasped and grabbed for the phone. "Don't say that. He might believe it. He already has it in his head that I'm to blame for two bodies being on the cliff this morning. I don't want him thinking my grandfather is some hit man."

Hugh returned his cell to his pocket. "I hope he takes me serious. Wilber isn't a guy you want to toy with. Not if you want to keep your head on your shoulders."

"Now you're just being silly. Grandpa is so

sweet. He's always hugging me and is always worried about me."

"*You* get hugs. The rest of us could get hunted."

"Maybe he's trying to solve the murders too," she said with a laugh, ignoring his comment on being hunted. It was hard to picture her grandfather running around town like a Hardy Boy. That didn't seem his style in the least. She frowned. "I never heard him come in today. I wonder why he didn't come into the shop?"

"He was probably going out to lay a world of hurt on someone."

She eyed him. "He's the sweetest man I know. I'm not sure his world of hurt would amount to much."

"Are you telling me you don't know what he is? What you both are?" Hugh asked, disbelief on his handsome face.

"I'm not following the question. What do you mean?" she inquired, at a loss to what he was refer- ring to.

He rubbed the bridge of his nose. "Penelope, do you know your family's history here in Everlasting?"

"I know that my grandfather's family has lived here for generations. I think they were part of the first group of settlers here."

"Yes, they were," he said evenly. "What else do you know of them?"

"Not much. Well, unless you count the crazy

stories my grandfather would tell me as a child. Stories of hunting mythical creatures and policing things that go bump in the night." It took all of her to say the words. She'd spent so many years defending Grandpa Wil from her mother's parents that she didn't like talking about him in a way that might paint him in a mentally unstable light.

When Hugh didn't laugh, she stepped back. He didn't honestly believe those stories, did he? There was no way any of the things her grandfather spoke of were real. No way at all.

"Penelope, what if I were to tell you that your grandfather isn't crazy? That his stories are true?"

"I'd wonder about your sanity. Grandpa has a really active imagination and is a great storyteller. I don't think for a minute that witches, werewolves, and vampires are real. Do you?"

"Oh, you'd be shocked by what I'm willing to believe," he said, moving a foot slightly, looking incredibly uncomfortable with the direction of the conversation.

She watched him for a sign he was joking but found none. "So you do believe in it all?"

He nodded.

Great. He was super attractive and insane.

"I bet you think the lighthouse is haunted too," she said with a snort.

"Yes. I know it is, but Cornelius doesn't show himself to men. Only women. That means I've never seen him for myself, but I know enough people who have. Plus, 'weird' is sort of Everlasting's middle name. A ghost is pretty tame compared to most of what goes on around here."

He really did believe it all. Who was this man? Did others in Everlasting share his views? Maybe the water was tainted or something. Or maybe they were all nuts.

She reached out and touched the back of a kitchen chair, feeling lightheaded. "I think I need to sit down."

Hugh pulled the chair out for her, and she took a seat. He grabbed another chair and moved it close to hers, taking a seat himself. He then gathered her hands in his, his gaze meeting hers. "There are a lot of things in Everlasting that are hard to explain to outsiders."

"I was born here," she said flatly.

He tipped his head and then his eyes widened. "I just put together who you are."

She stilled.

"We played together as kids," he said, quirking a smile in her direction. "I'm pretty sure I cried when you moved away, but let's keep that tidbit to ourselves, okay?"

She hiccupped as she laughed. "Deal."

"It's good to see you smile. I was worried me telling you the truth about the town would freak you out."

"Oh, you're totally freaking me out with that, but I'm choosing to believe that your mind is a bit muddled because I hit you with my car this morning."

He exhaled, still holding her hands. "Penelope, it's important you listen and that you believe me. There are a number of people in this town who fear your grandfather and have a bone to pick with him. For good reason. I don't want you hurt because of that."

"Everyone's been nice so far. Well, except Deputy March. He's convinced I'm a serial killer," she said softly.

"Ignore Jake." Hugh cleared his throat. "Trust me. News has spread all over town that Wilber's granddaughter is here. It's just a matter of time before some moron decides to try to have a go at you because they're too afraid of Wilber to go at *him*."

She eyed him cautiously. "Who in the world would be afraid of Grandpa? Other than you."

"Anyone with a brain in their head," he replied. "He's far more than he appears to be. So are you."

She shook her head. "I'm the type of person who trips over their own feet. I'm not a danger to anyone. Well, unless they don't look before crossing and walk out into the street in front of me."

He grinned. "I've never been happier to be hit by a car in my life."

"That has happened to you before?" she questioned.

He nodded. "Once or twice."

"Hold the pickles," she breathed, making him laugh. "How are you alive?"

"It's hard to keep a good man down," he said before squeezing her hand gently. "But then again, I'm more than a man."

She watched him.

Chapter Twelve

Hugh had never told anyone about himself. Those who knew him in town had known all along what he was, what his family was. Telling Penelope the truth was a huge deal. But it felt right. Like he had to make sure she understood what he really was. "I'm a wolf-shifter."

She just stared at him as if she were waiting for the punch line. Sadly, there wasn't one. The truth hung there between them for what felt like an eternity. When it became clear that she wasn't going to say anything, he decided to fill the void.

"That means I can turn into a wolf at will and that once a month, I'm left no choice but to change shapes," he said, wanting to drive the point home. He waited with bated breath, sure she'd scream and maybe throw something at him. She might even run in terror, fearful he'd eat her.

She just sat there.

"Penelope?" he asked, concerned he'd perhaps broken her.

A small laugh bubbled up from her before it moved into a full-blown cackle. She bent forward, holding on to him for support as she continued to laugh to the point she cried. "Oh my stars. I went from a man who didn't see me as worthy to a man who is delusional. Wow. I have no luck with men."

Hugh absorbed what she was saying, and anger welled in him. "Who didn't see you as worthy? Tell me his name, and I'll handle him for you. I'll take him out and show him where a bear goes in the woods."

He cringed as one of Petey's favorite threats fell free from his lips. Polly's spell was more like a curse.

She laughed more. "Now you sound like Grandpa. He threatened to break Craig's legs."

Hugh tensed. He didn't appreciate being likened to Wilber Messing. "Penelope, can we please talk about what I just told you? About me being a wolf-shifter?"

"Wolf-shifter? Really? Let me guess, Curt thinks he's a leprechaun. Does Buster think he's a butter-fly? Oh, I bet Petey changes into a sea lion. Does Sigmund change into a hawk?"

Hugh licked his lower lip. "Uh, no. Curt is a lion-shifter."

Her laughter reached epic proportions. She fanned her face with her hand. "Stop. I'm going to wet myself."

Hugh found himself chuckling, finding her refreshing. "Sigmund comes from a line of were-marine creatures, each one in his family is different. We aren't sure why he's not shown any signs of being able to shift forms. Buster is a were-rat. Petey is a wolf-shifter, same as me."

Penelope almost fell out of the chair as she continued to laugh. "Were-rat? For the love of all that is purple, you have got the best imagination out there. I thought Grandpa was a great storyteller. You might have him beat."

"It's all true, Penelope. And your grandfather comes from a long line of hunters. Men and women who kill my kind and police them."

Penelope stopped laughing. "This story isn't very funny anymore."

"No. It's not," stated Hugh evenly.

She sat up straight. "You really think my grandpa is capable of hurting someone?"

"Yes. And so are you if you want the truth. It's in your blood," he returned.

"I didn't hit you with my car on purpose. We've been over this." She sat back in the chair.

"I know. I'm not saying you did. I'm saying, if you ever had to protect yourself from real danger, I think you could more than handle yourself. But I'm also not willing to risk your life. Until we figure out who the dead men are and what happened to them, I'd feel better if you stayed close to me or your grandfather."

She met his gaze and held it. "You really think you can turn into a wolf."

"Honey, I don't just think it, I know it. I can show you when you're ready. Trust me, you're not ready yet."

She nodded. "You're right. I'm so not ready for that."

"How about we head down to the marina, and we can take one of my boats out to the location the bodies were found. Maybe we'll find something there that the police missed."

"I have a confession to make," she said.

"What's that?"

"I've never been on a boat."

He grinned. "Just think, you'll be on a boat with a wolf-shifter."

She giggled, and it was clear she didn't believe him. He couldn't blame her. It was hard to wrap one's mind around it all. "Because they're known for loving ocean swims."

"Oh yeah. We love a good midnight ocean dip. Sometimes, we even like to swim without clothes on." Hugh winked suggestively.

Instantly, her cheeks flamed with red. "Keep your clothes on please. At least for now."

For now? That meant there was hope he'd get to undress with her at some point. He could work with that.

Chapter Thirteen

Hugh released Penelope's hand as they came around the corner of Petey's bait shop and found Petey on the largest of Hugh's sailboats. Petey gave a small wave and pushed a cooler into the cockpit area. "Uh, Petey, what are you doing?"

Petey glanced up at him. "Helping you out. You're hopeless on your own. Trust me, you need all the assistance we're willing to give."

"We're?" Hugh asked, walking toward the docks.

Buster walked up into the cockpit area from below deck. He glanced over and spotted Hugh. The man then looked up at the setting sun, and started to whistle, as if that would avoid attention being drawn to him.

"Guys, what are you doing?" demanded Hugh.

Next up from below was Curt, dressed in a pair of Dockers and a long-sleeved V-neck sweater. He beamed as he spotted Hugh. "Great. You managed to convince her to join you. That's a good thing, or this could have been really awkward."

"From my point of view, it still is awkward," said Hugh, waiting for an explanation as to what the men were doing on his personal sailboat.

Curt continued to smile. "We took care of dinner for you two tonight. And the boat is all set for you to take her out."

Petey looked up. "It's gonna be a great night. Lots of stars. Very romantic. Try not to ruin it, Hugh."

Buster continued to whistle and avoid eye contact.

Curt laughed. "Sigmund was going to help, but his allergies started acting up more so he's taking more meds and is staying in for the rest of the night. He sends his best and wants to stress that you need to not screw this up with Penelope."

Petey smiled wide. "Yeppers. He said that it's rare to find a woman who can tolerate your temper."

A giggle came from Penelope. "He's really very delicate and non-threatening. You should have seen him on the fainting sofa."

All the men snorted, Hugh included. He took

her hand in his once more and led her to the boat. "I'm afraid to see what these three cooked up."

"Hey, we didn't do any cooking," said Petey. He thumbed toward Curt. "He had his chef do the cooking. We just did the heavy lifting and made it special."

Hugh glanced at Penelope, worried his friends, while well meaning, would chase her off. She was all smiles as she allowed him to help her onto the sailboat.

Buster and Petey were on her in an instant, talking her ear off as Curt pulled Hugh aside. "Dinner for two has been provided. There is cheese-cake in there as well. And wine. Don't do anything I wouldn't do."

Hugh nodded and clasped Curt's hand, pulling him into their version of a manly hug. "Thanks, man."

"No problem. Just be careful out there. When you told me you wanted to take her to the spot the bodies were found, I thought you were nuts. Then I realized you just wanted alone time on the boat with her."

Hugh glanced in the direction Petey and Buster had pulled Penelope off in. He lowered his voice. "I told her the truth about me."

"That you're a jerk?" asked Curt, snorting. "News flash. That isn't a secret, Lupine."

Hugh growled lightly. "No. That I'm a wolf-shifter."

Curt's eyes widened. "Did she freak?"

"She laughed. A lot. I don't think she believed me."

"Not really a shock. Hard to soak in. Though I'd have thought Wil would have told her the truth about supernaturals," said Curt.

Hugh nodded. "I think he tried but did it in the form of bedtime stories. Penelope has grown up thinking everything strange in Everlasting is simply a made-up story."

Curt exhaled loudly. "Good luck with everything tonight. And be careful. Remember, something killed those men, and the murderer hasn't been found. Unless, you're having a romantic dinner with her, alone, on the boat tonight."

Hugh snorted. "She wouldn't hurt anyone."

"I noticed you didn't say she couldn't hurt anyone. We all know what the Messings can do when push comes to shove," added Curt. "I don't really think she had anything to do with what happened by the cliffs, but that doesn't mean she's harmless. Be careful. As much as you get on my nerves, I like you alive."

"Aww, that is the sweetest thing you've ever said to me."

Curt offered a cocky smile. "Well, it is nicer than being called a fish stick."

"Eat a muffin, lemon head," said Hugh, instantly regretting it.

"Polly is awesome!" Curt laughed. He brought his hand up for a high-five that went unreturned by Hugh. "Totally worth losing the bet to hear this. I hope you get fleas again."

Hugh gave Curt a hard shove, and the man nearly fell overboard.

In the blink of an eye, Penelope was there, catching hold of Curt, steadying him as if the man weighed nothing. Curt was the same size as Hugh. The strength she'd had to use to complete the act was supernatural worthy. Something a born hunter could easily do.

Both men shared a knowing look.

Penelope pointed a finger at Hugh. "I saw you push him. Shame on you. He was out here with Petey and Buster doing something nice for you and me, and the thanks he gets is that?"

Lowering his head, Hugh put his hands behind his back, feeling like a scolded child. "Sorry. Won't happen again."

"It better not," she warned.

Curt laughed and gave Buster a light jab on the arm. "This is great. I hope she sends him to his room."

"Keep it up, and I'll push you in and save him the time," she said to Curt, making Buster and Petey laugh.

"I really like her," offered Buster, adjusting his bow tie.

"Come on," said Petey. "Let's leave these two young lovebirds to start their evening. I'm off to check on Polly. Gotta make sure she knows I was thinking of her."

"Has she forgiven you for the fishing lure corsage yet?" asked Buster, walking behind Petey to the edge of the boat.

"Kind of," admitted Petey. "Okay, not really. I thought it was a thing of beauty. She loved Herman."

"Herman?" asked Penelope.

Hugh glanced at her. "A live lobster that Petey gave her to eat. She kept it as a pet and named it."

Penelope walked over to the older man and planted a chaste kiss on his cheek. "Thank you for everything, Petey. I'm sure I'm going to love it."

Petey blushed. "Aw shucks. You're welcome. I'm just doing my part to get Hugh married off. The boy doesn't stand a chance on his own."

She laughed. "That is a big job."

"Don't I know it. No pain. No gain," said Petey, hopping off the boat with the skill of a seasoned fisherman. "Let's get this show on the road, folks."

Buster was next to get off, but he wasn't quite as accomplished as Petey and nearly fell off the other side of the dock and into the water. Petey caught him and held him still.

"Steady, mate," said Petey.

Buster gulped. "I can't swim."

"I know," said Petey.

Curt patted Hugh on the shoulder and exited the boat as well, leaving Hugh standing alone with Penelope. He couldn't help but think of kissing her again. Of what her lips had felt like against his. His body tightened, and he had to swallow down a groan of frustration. The woman would be his downfall if he wasn't careful. She'd been back in his life a day, and already he felt a connection to her unlike any other person. He couldn't even think what tomorrow might bring. If he could keep from sticking his foot in his mouth, he just might be gifted another date with her. First, he had to get through this one without doing anything to annoy her—something he seemed terribly good at.

"Are you still okay with all of this?" he asked, wanting to be sure she was happy. "I can have one of them come too if you're uncomfortable in any way."

A huge smile moved over her beautiful face. "I trust you, Hugh. I think you're nuts, but I trust you. Now, let's go find out what really happened by the cliffs and then you're feeding me, remember?"

"Yes ma'am," he said, giving a small salute. He lifted a seat on the deck and pulled out a life jacket. Hugh held it out to Penelope. "Here. Put this on."

"I can swim. I just haven't been on a boat before."

Against his better judgment, Hugh put the life jacket back under one of the seats. He'd feel a hell of a lot better if she was wearing the thing, but he didn't want to push the issue.

Chapter Fourteen

"How many boats do you have?" asked Penelope as Hugh brought the large sailboat to a stop near a rocky shoreline that butted against a cliff face. There looked to be a flat section on the rocks, but from her vantage point, she couldn't see how far back it extended.

She could see the edge of the road above that she'd been on earlier in the day when the storms had come through. It had seemed high when she was on it. From below she got a sense of just how high up it truly was.

She gulped, happy with her choice to stop when the weather got too bad rather than risk plummeting to her death.

Hugh eased up alongside her. "This is the spot I was told the bodies were found."

She looked around. "There isn't any police tape or anything here. Are you sure?"

"Everlasting doesn't always do things the ways other places do. Trust me. I'm right. I'm picking up a lot of scents here. That means a large number of people were here very recently. I can smell Deputy March, the sheriff, the county medical examiner, and some other locals. Plus some people I don't know."

She didn't question him about what he smelled, afraid he'd launch into the whole wolf-shifter thing again, ruining their date night with irrational talk. "How am I going to prove I didn't do this?"

"It will all work itself out in the end. It always does," he said, putting an arm around her gently.

Somehow, his words helped to ease some of the worry. She didn't want to believe she could end up in trouble for a crime she didn't commit, but she'd heard stories of people who really were innocent being imprisoned. Some spent decades behind bars. Could that happen to her too? The thought was terrifying.

As if sensing she was about to spiral into a mess of anxiety, Hugh squeezed her tighter. It was exactly what she needed.

She sank into his warm embrace, surprised at just how chilly the air was on the water. Her puppy dog sweater wasn't warm enough for the falling temperature, and her light jacket was in her checked bags. She hadn't thought to grab it before leaving her grandfather's house. "I hope you're right. All I wanted to do was get away from Chicago and Craig and clear my head. I certainly never thought I'd be staring prison in the face because of it."

Hugh tensed, his muscles bulging as he held her against his body. "Tell me about this Craig."

Twisting in his arms, she expelled a slow breath and faced him. "Craig and I were a couple for two years. He'd always been embarrassed by my clothing choices, by my lack of ambition at work, and by my personality. As I look back, I'm not sure why he was with me at all. Then, one day, he decided I wasn't marriage material, and he was ready to settle down and start a family—just not with me. He dumped me and within no time at all he was engaged to someone else. I was really broken up about it. In truth, that is why I came to Everlasting. I was hoping to forget my troubles. Looks like new trouble found me."

"And now?" he asked softly, though a dangerous note hung in his voice. "Are you still broken up about it all?"

She slid her arms around his waist and put her head to his chest. She could remain there forever, just letting him hold her. There was something about him that made her feel not only safe but as if she were home. "Not as much as I had been this morning. You know, before I was a murder suspect."

His deep laugh reverberated through his chest, sending shivers of desire down her spine. "You're a person of interest, that's all."

"That's all?" she echoed. "I don't even jaywalk let alone murder people."

"I jaywalk all the time," he said, still laughing.

She tipped her head back to get a better view of his face. "I know. I hit you with my car when you were doing it."

"Pretty much the only way to knock sense into me," he admitted with a wink.

She chuckled and hugged him again, their closeness causing desire to thrum beneath her skin. "It's getting dark. Should we head back?"

"We could, or we could eat," Hugh said, stepping back from her. "Curt, Petey, and Buster went all out for us. They aren't really known for being date facilitators, so I say we enjoy their hard work. I'll pull up anchor, and we can head down just a bit to find a better spot to eat. Sound good?"

"Is it wrong that I'm a little scared to see what they think is dinner?" she asked, positive Curt would think something super fancy would be to her liking. It wouldn't. She was a meat-and-potatoes kind of girl. And she'd seen what Petey liked to eat—Polly had named it and thought of it as a pet.

Hugh stared at her for the longest time before he spoke. "Honey, you should know that I think you're marriage material."

She gasped.

He looked as stunned by his statement as she was. "Fish sticks with ketchup," he blurted before hurrying off. The man certainly had offbeat sayings.

Penelope followed behind him and touched his back lightly, stopping him from pulling up the anchor. "Let's just have our dinner here."

His gaze moved in the direction of the rocky shoreline. "Are you sure? I can take you to that cove I told you about."

"Hugh, it's fine. There is no evidence here of what happened. And we're pretty far out from the shoreline still."

Nodding, he stood tall. "There are rocks below. The closer you get to the shore, the worse they are. It's not smart to take a boat any closer. You risk hull damage and sinking."

"Here is perfect." Going to her tiptoes, she kissed his scruffy cheek. "Thank you for being so considerate. And thanks for not being too mad that I hit you with my car."

"Honey, if I'd have known I'd get to be on a boat and have a star-filled dinner with you on the ocean, I'd have let you back over me with that tiny thing you keep calling a car."

She laughed. "I'm almost afraid to ask what you drive."

"A gas-guzzling truck," he returned with a cocky grin.

"Why am I not surprised?"

A smug expression was her only answer from him before he kissed her forehead quickly, then darted off, going below. He came up with a basket and a blanket. Artfully, he made his way to the deck and laid the blanket out. For as muscular and tall as he was, he moved with a fluid grace around the sailboat, as if he'd been born on it. He set the basket on the edge of the blanket and then shocked her by coming back for her.

"Here," he said, holding out his hand. He walked her to the deck, making sure she had her footing under her the entire way. He didn't release her hand until she was seated on the blanket.

It was so sweet that she couldn't help but think of her time with Craig. He'd never been so thoughtful, and he'd never bothered to do anything even close to romantic for her.

The longer she was around Hugh, the more she began to wonder what she had been thinking being with Craig. At the rate she was going, she wouldn't even remember Craig's name come morning.

That was her hope anyway.

Hugh hurried off and returned frowning, holding up a bottle of whiskey. "This was chilling where the wine should be. My guess, Petey changed out the wine for this."

Penelope snorted. It was easy to picture Petey

doing that very thing. "I'll have water if you don't mind. I'm not really much of a drinker."

"Water it is," he said, walking off again only to return with two bottles of cold water. He sat down next to her and opened the picnic basket. Tossing his head back, he laughed—and then pulled out peanut butter and jelly sandwiches, and an assortment of other goodies.

Penelope took one. "Oh, I love these. I was worried it would be something I couldn't pronounce. I'm not fancy at all."

He handed her a note from the basket.

She read it and couldn't stop smiling from ear to ear. The men had thought to put in peanut butter and jelly sandwiches because of Hugh's newfound non-cursing status. They'd even added a box of frozen fish sticks, but Petey had a postscript on the note warning them not to eat them because they didn't smell natural. Thankfully, the men had also sent Italian pasta salad and a meat and cheese tray, along with assorted olives.

Penelope went right for the olives, having always had a soft spot for them. She thought of them as comfort food and whenever she was stressed she tended to eat them by the handfuls. They ate in relative silence, looking up as the sun set fully and the sky darkened. It was beautiful.

Hugh ate the sandwiches and then helped

himself to pasta salad. He put some on a plate and held it out for her. "Here. Eat more."

She touched her stomach. "I can't. I ate a ton."

"You ate like a bird. Eat up," he said, pushing pasta salad at her. He wasn't taking no for answer.

She picked at it, eating a mozzarella ball before moving around the cherry tomatoes, pieces of meat, black Greek olives, and crumbled feta cheese, unable to get much down because she'd single-handedly eaten almost all the meat and cheese tray, not to mention she'd put a dent in the olive reserve too. As delicious as the pasta salad was, she couldn't eat any more.

"Ready for cheesecake?" asked Hugh, a wolfish grin spreading over his face. He patted his nonexistent gut. "I'm still starving."

She stared at him, her jaw agape. He'd polished off a large amount of food and didn't show any signs of slowing. "Where do you put everything you eat? You're nothing but muscle. Not an ounce of fat on you."

"Shifters have high metabolisms," he said nonchalantly. "We eat a lot every day. We have to."

"Uh-huh, sure they do," she answered, nearly laughing at his humor. He really was running with the whole joke of being supernatural. She had to hand it to him, his made-up reality was well thought out.

He touched her hand tenderly and heat flared

through her skin. "Penelope, eventually you're going to have to listen to me with both ears and know I'm not joking."

"Try to see it from my perspective," she said, keeping her hand in place, enjoying his touch. "You expect me to believe that you can do the impossible. That you can change shapes into an animal. That's a lot to swallow for anyone. And that is only the tip of the iceberg. Ghosts, shifters, and who knows what else are real as well?"

"Yes. So are witches. The devil is real too. I can introduce you to him if you want. Nice guy," he returned. "Mrs. Mays is another matter. Avoid her. She can scare the hair off a dog with her glares."

Penelope grabbed a stray olive and ate it. She might be full but she needed a coping mechanism, and the olive was it. "I'm almost afraid to ask who is a witch in town. Jolene?"

"No. She's a were-dolphin." He delivered the news as if he were telling her something as mundane as someone's eye color.

"Of course she is." Penelope found herself listening, totally enraptured, much like she used to be when she was little, and her grandfather would tell her similar stories about Everlasting and the people who lived there.

Hugh sighed, his frustration with her showing. "Polly and Anna from Witch's Brew Coffee Shop & Bakery are witches. There are more in town too. All of them are good, so don't fear them. They haven't dropped a house on anyone—that I know of."

She leaned against him. "Dorothy was the one who dropped a house on a witch. A witch didn't drop a house on anyone in *The Wizard of Oz.*"

Hugh rubbed his jawline. "Huh. Learn something new every day. My childhood was full of the real thing, so I didn't pay much attention to movies about it all."

"And my grandfather is a hunter of them all?" she asked, doing her best to avoid laughing at him. He looked so serious, and like he truly bought into what he was saying.

With a nod, he drew back and stood. "He is. He claims he gave it up years ago, when your father and mother passed, but a leopard doesn't change its spots."

Penelope tensed at the mention of her parents' passing.

Hugh bent and went to one knee near her. He pushed her long hair back from her face. His expression was guarded. "Hey, I'm sorry. I shouldn't have brought that up. I was just trying to give you a timeline of when Wilber hung up his hunting gear, or rather when he claimed he did."

She mulled over what he was saying. As great as a world filled with magic and mystery sounded, the real world wasn't like that. It was a hard place, where sorrow and heartbreak lived. There were no magic potions or spells to fix everything wrong in one's life. There was simply reality, and it often sucked. "I was little when my parents died. I've come to terms with it over the years. And I know they wouldn't have wanted me to wallow for the rest of my life."

"No. I don't think they would have wanted that at all," Hugh said, remaining close to her. "I'm guessing your father would have lectured you about having dinner with me," he said with a grin. "I remember him chasing me out of your backyard more than once when we were little. Your mom liked me. She used to swat his arm and tell him to stop and to let us be. She was a sweet lady, not to mention she was beautiful. Like you."

Sadness tightened her chest. "You remember my parents better than I do. Mostly, I remember walking in their funeral procession. I have very few memories before that all, but that day sticks with me."

"I remember more about them because I'm four years older than you," he said, caressing her cheek. "I can still remember the day your other grandparents drove off with you. I chased after their car. Though, I will say, I remember calling you Penny, not Penelope."

She perked. He'd done that? She hadn't remembered. Then again, she didn't really remember him from her childhood.

"My father and my uncle even went to your grandfather, trying to help him keep you here in Everlasting. Let me tell you what that meant for two of my pack, who are blood relations, to seek out a hunter and try to help him. It didn't work out, but more than one person wanted you to stay. I know Wilber wanted it too."

She frowned. "I didn't want to go. My choices weren't my own then. My grandparents thought they were doing the right thing. Grandpa Wil liked to talk about supernatural things. My other grandparents thought he wasn't stable enough to be left in charge of me. And they felt they could do a better job raising a little girl than he could."

"Were they good to you?" asked Hugh.

"Very. They still are. I see them once a year around the holidays," she said. "They weren't thrilled when Grandpa Wil and I reconnected, but I'm an adult now, so my choices are my own."

He rose to his feet and managed to stay upright when the boat rocked back and forth slightly. It was easy to see he was used to being on a boat and the ocean. "Cheesecake time."

She snorted. "I'm not hungry. Stuff me full of anything else, and I'll pop."

Groaning, he stared at her, looking hopeful.

She snickered and tipped over on her side. "Your mind is in the gutter."

"Normally my words are too. I'm afraid to tell

you what I'm thinking right now. It will end up sounding like I have a baked good fetish or something. Polly's potion will be my greatest downfall."

She cackled with laughter as he hurried off to retrieve the cheesecake.

Chapter Fifteen

Hugh put a piece of creamy, fresh cheesecake on a plate for Penelope and then spooned a gooey cranberry topping over it. No way was he putting that on his. He hated cranberries, and they were everywhere in Everlasting this time of year.

No thank you.

The smell of them even turned his stomach.

It took him a minute to realize he was smiling hard enough to cause his face to crack. Having Penelope near him made him happy. Happier than he'd been in his life, but he couldn't explain why. She just felt right. Like she was supposed to be close to him.

"Calm down, Lupine," he said in a hushed tone to himself. "She's been in your life a day now. Take it slow."

He made his way back to the topside, a plate of

cheesecake in each hand. The moment his feet touched the deck the boat tilted hard to the right, causing Hugh to drop the cheesecake. He righted himself and scanned the water, wondering if a larger boat had come past when he wasn't paying attention, leaving a big wake behind.

There was no sign of anything.

They were alone.

"Penelope?" he asked, worried if she was okay. The boat had rocked hard enough to cause him to lose his footing, and he was a seasoned vet.

"I didn't fall in if that's what you're wondering," she said, setting his mind at ease.

"I hereby forbid you from falling in. Got it?" he said, only partially joking. As the thought of her actually falling overboard came over him, panic welled. His palms began to sweat, and for half a second, he feared he'd lose control of his wolf and change shapes then and there—no matter if she was prepared for the sight or not. After a few tense seconds, he gathered control of himself once more and looked at the cheesecake on the boat. There was no salvaging it. Perfectly good dessert was now smashed and would require a good rinse down with a hose when he got back to the marina. "Fish sticks."

He groaned, inwardly cursing Polly.

Penelope laughed loudly from the deck.

"Our cheesecake died a horrible death!" he called out.

She laughed more. "Tell Deputy March I was innocent in its ending."

He snorted and was about to say something witty when the boat rocked hard again; this time it was very clear something had struck the hull of the boat. And whatever it was, it wasn't small. It hit the boat again and caused it to tip with a force that sent Hugh sliding across the cockpit area. He caught himself on the lifeline and only barely managed to stay on the boat. For a split second, he worried they'd capsize.

This wasn't an area you wanted to be in the water. The currents would bash a body against the unforgiving rocks of the shoreline. While he'd be able to survive that kind of damage and heal, he wasn't sure Penelope would. There was no way he wanted to test the theory.

Penelope's scream clawed at his gut, and he shot up and across the boat, drawing on his supernatural speed. He was to the deck in less than a second, grabbing her and drawing her back from the edge. He kept hold of her as the boat rocked violently. She cried out again as the picnic basket tumbled over the edge and into the ocean. Hugh didn't care about it. His only worry was Penelope.

He moved her quickly in the direction of the cockpit, wanting to get her in a life jacket before he did anything else. He couldn't stomach the idea of her falling in and being lost at sea. In that instant, he knew he'd move heaven and hell for the dark-haired beauty in his arms. The idea should have stopped him dead in his tracks, but adrenaline and fear for her safety kept him going.

Once they made it to the cockpit, he grabbed a life jacket and clumsily managed to get it on her before rushing back to the wheel. "Go below!"

"Hugh!" shouted Penelope, ignoring his order, as the boat continued to rock in a manner it shouldn't. The swells were small, and there was no bad weather.

Something was under them, striking the boat again and again. That wasn't something that usually happened. Whales and sharks didn't attack boats despite what the movies wanted people to believe. The thought sobered him instantly.

He was just about to grab the wheel when something came up from the ocean and over the side of the boat at him. It took his mind a moment to comprehend what he was seeing—a giant tentacle. It wrapped around him faster than he could move away and in one powerful motion, it ripped him over the side and into the icy depths of the ocean. The cold water nearly stole the air from his lungs.

He'd grown up on the ocean. He didn't fear it, but he did respect it. And right now, he knew he was screwed. Whatever had him had a vise-like grip around his waist. The fact that it was causing him internal injuries meant something. Whatever it was, it was very powerful.

Hugh let his shifter side poke through as claws erected from his fingertips. He slashed at the tentacle around him. The minute the creature loosened its hold he kicked his feet, following the bubbles upward. His sole concern was Penelope. Had whatever grabbed him gotten her too? He broke the surface and sucked in a huge breath of air. The boat was about twenty feet from him now. He spotted Penelope there, looking over the edge of the boat, terror on her beautiful face.

Relief swept through him.

She was safe.

He started to swim in the direction of the boat. He'd only taken a few strokes when he found himself being yanked under the surface again. With his claws still extended, he thrashed at the sea creature, all the while trying to keep his head about him. Panicking would cause him to lose air faster than he was able to take it in and would only serve to kill him faster.

He cut deep into the tentacle, and the creature released him once again. Hugh didn't even make it to the surface for another breath before another tentacle caught him around the ankle, yanking him toward the creature, and holding him underwater even longer. It was then he got a good look at the thing attacking him.

For a moment, his mind couldn't compute what he was seeing. It wasn't an octopus or a giant squid. It was something he'd seen in paintings, depicted in old books the town kept on the history of supernatural beings and the strange and unusual.

What held him underwater was something even he had a hard time believing was real—a kraken.

Great time to panic now.

He somehow managed to maintain his cool, despite wanting to yell. He came face to face with the beast and found himself looking into a set of eyes that instantly made him think of his friend Sigmund.

That was absurd.

Sigmund didn't troll the seas and try to drown people. He just sneezed a lot.

The creature jerked harder on Hugh, and Hugh's lungs screamed in agony. As the creature opened its mouth, showing rows of jagged teeth, Hugh knew the end was near.

Just then, a streak of red light shot right past him, striking the creature. It reared back, releasing him in the process. Hugh lunged for the surface and sucked in a huge breath, his lungs burning.

He coughed and then got his senses about him and swam quickly in the direction of the boat. He made it back in record time. As he reached up to pull himself from the water, Penelope's hand wrapped around his wrist. She gave a hard yank, stunning him by not only lifting his entire body weight out of the water with one fluid motion, but also flinging him onto the deck with a hard thud, knocking the wind out of him.

Blackness swarmed his vision. One second he was looking up at the sky and the next he was out cold.

Chapter Sixteen

"Holy Hannah! He's dead!" shouted Penelope. Her heart beat madly as she slid on the deck to Hugh. She instantly launched into life-saving measures. Although she wasn't exactly sure how to perform CPR. She'd never taken a course on it. She'd seen it done on television. Anyone could do it, right?

She put her mouth to his and was just about to blow in a breath of air when Hugh's tongue greeted hers. His hand slid into the back of her hair, and he held her head in place, his tongue still teasing hers. Somehow, she didn't think this was part of the process.

She pushed on his chest. As much as she wanted the kiss to go on, she needed to know he was totally all right.

They broke apart slightly. "Hey there," he said, a lopsided grin on his face.

"Are you hurt?"

"My pride is damaged because you tossed me onto the boat like a rag doll, but other than that, I'm good. Is the Kraken still gone?"

She let out a long breath that she hadn't been aware she'd been holding. "Thank Juniper. Wait? Kraken? As in, you know, a Kraken?"

"You have very strange sayings," he said.

"This from the man who used 'fish sticks' as a curse word."

He grinned at her more, and she bent, planting a chaste kiss on his lips. "Thank you."

She stayed close to him, noticing that he wasn't freezing like he should have been coming from the cold water. If anything, he was extra hot. She blinked a few times and then his earlier statement began to sink in. "Hold the pickles. Were you serious about that huge octopus thing being a kraken?"

"Yes," said Hugh. "And I'd like you to know I'm very fond of pickles."

She stared down at him. Was he for real? Yes, whatever had attacked the boat and Hugh had been massive and had a lot of tentacles, but a kraken? No. That couldn't be. They weren't real.

Neither are werewolves, ghosts, and witches, but that doesn't stop him from talking about them.

He'd been underwater a long time. More than a person ever should. Perhaps he was suffering from lack of oxygen. That would explain what he was saying and what he thought he saw. She didn't know much about oxygen deprivation, but she'd go out on a limb that hallucinations might be a side effect.

"We need to get you to a hospital," she said, trying to lift his weight from the deck. She couldn't budge him. She'd pulled him over the side only minutes before, but now he was like trying to move a mountain.

He tugged on her, pulling her down to him, his mouth finding hers. His kiss was tender yet packed full of need. Her concern for him took root, and she found herself returning the kiss with equal amounts of worry and eagerness. Hugh met her all the way. When they finally drew back from one another, they were both breathless.

"I need to nearly drown more often," he said, a goofy look on his face.

She swatted at his arm. "Not funny."

"Ouch," he said, rubbing his arm, his eyes widened. "Woman, you are really strong."

She frowned. "I'm not."

"You pulled me onto this boat with one hand and I more than cleared the rail. I told you that you had the ability to do great things."

She shook her head. "That was just the adrenaline. Mothers lift cars off children when in crisis mode. There isn't anything supernatural about it. I just tried to get you off the deck and couldn't budge you. See. I'm normal. So are you. Well, you can hold your breath a long time and live to tell the tale, but other than that you're relatively sane."

Relatively being the keyword.

The boat rocked again, and Hugh pushed to his feet. He grabbed her, putting her body behind his in a protective manner as he stared out at the water, illuminated only by partial moonlight. She couldn't see much beyond blackness, but Hugh didn't appear to be having issues. The man must have incredible night vision.

The tension in his body eased, and he stopped crowding her behind him and turned to face her. He looked to the side at the flare gun on the deck. "You shot it, didn't you?"

She nodded. "I almost jumped in after you, but figured whatever that was had a lot of legs so having us both trapped wouldn't help anyone. It was then I looked for something to use as a weapon. Let me just say that worked far better than a ballpoint pen, which was my last go-to weapon choice."

"Huh?" he asked, confusion coating his face.

"Nothing," she said, thinking back to how she'd clutched a ballpoint pen in her rental car, on the edge of the cliffs above, thinking the end was near. It turned out to be only Jolene.

The boat stopped rocking and stilled. Everything seemed incredibly calm as if nothing had occurred there. Had she not just been part of it, she'd have never believed any of it *had* occurred.

Her first day in Everlasting was certainly turning out to be memorable.

She and Hugh stared at one another for what felt like an eternity. Finally, Hugh leaned over the side of the boat and boldly stared down at the water.

Penelope grabbed the belt loop of his jeans and held firm. She didn't want him to be a snack for whatever that thing was.

He stepped back. "It's gone. At least for now."

"W-what was it, for real?"

He faced her. "The truth or a lie to soften it all?"

"Truth," she said.

"I already told you the truth. It was a kraken."

Penelope's blood went cold. She blinked several times and thought harder about everything that had happened since her arrival in Everlasting in the wee hours of the morning. As it all sank in, she felt light-headed. She'd seen the creature with her own eyes. It wasn't something found in nature. There was no logical explanation for it. At least nothing that made sense.

"Hugh."

"Yeah, hon?" he asked, his voice low as if he knew she was close to being in a state of shock.

"Can you show me the shifter side of you now?"

As he stood before her his arms suddenly

sprouted gray fur. As if that wasn't enough, long claws sprang forth from his fingertips. His already large, muscular arms seemed to increase in size and mass. She looked up to find his brown gaze was now an icy blue.

"Hold the pickles," she mumbled before passing out.

Chapter Seventeen

Hugh continued to pace the floor of Warrick's Surf & Turf. Curt was close, pouring Hugh a three-finger shot of high-end bourbon. Seeing Curt using the good stuff, Pappy Van Winkle's, surprised him. Curt liked the finer things in life, but he also knew when to keep something back for a special occasion. Apparently, having his best friend nearly eaten by a kraken meant the good stuff was pulled out.

Hugh shook his head. "No. I need to keep my wits about me. Penelope isn't handling this well."

"To be fair, she was almost dinner for a kraken right before you decided to come out of the shifter closet." Curt looked past him in the direction of Penelope, who hadn't budged since coming to.

"It felt like the right time." Hugh ran a hand through his hair as he stood in the bar area of the fancy restaurant that Curt had opened nearly ten years back. It did well and seemed to be a favorite among not only the locals but tourists as well. Hugh wasn't a big fan of fancy foods, so he preferred Chickadee's Diner. Curt had a back area that he often rented out for wedding receptions, retirement parties, and so forth. The doors to that area were open, indicating the restaurant had been packed earlier and the overflow seating area had been needed.

"Answer something for me," said Curt, pushing the glass toward Hugh on the bar top. The surface was made from reclaimed wood. Hugh had helped Curt handcraft it when he'd opened the place. The wood had been from an old ship and gave a nod to the ocean and sailing—something Curt loved dearly. Both men did. "What made you want to tell her at all? You've dated plenty of women whom you never bothered to tell what you are. Why her and why the same day that you meet her?"

There was the rub. He'd known Penelope all his life. She'd been important to him when they were children and had somehow managed to become more important to him as an adult. He didn't know why. All he knew was that nothing would ever be the same for him again. She'd hit him with her car and spun his world on its axis. "I met her when we were kids. I just didn't put that together until later in the day."

"Cut the crap," said Curt with an incensed

breath. "You confessed something huge to a woman you barely know and who has been back in your life a day. I want to know why. There is a lot at stake telling someone about shifters, and you well know that. This is bigger than just you. Everlasting could be at risk. You know that we all agreed to keep what we are secret from outsiders."

"She's not an outsider. She was born here." Hugh lowered his head, his emotions all over the place. He'd not been able to think clearly since he'd looked up to see Penelope above him after she'd struck him with her car. "I don't know what came over me. I'm different with her."

"I noticed," returned Curt, a slightly amused note to his voice. "Hell, even Petey noticed and you've seen how good with the opposite sex he is."

Hugh glanced in the direction of Penelope, who was still sitting at a dining table with a blanket around her shoulders, staring at the candle that was lit on the table top. White linens covered each table, and fresh flowers were in small vases at each as well. Curt wasn't one to spare any expense when it came to his restaurant. He'd had custom artwork done with scenes depicting the local fishing and boating industry. Several of Hugh's charter boats were shown in the paintings.

"Think she snapped?" asked Curt, motioning to Penelope.

"To be honest, I'm not sure."

Penelope hadn't said a word since she'd woken when Hugh was docking the boat. Curt had walked out, getting ready to close up his restaurant for the night, and found Hugh carrying Penelope from the sailboat. When Hugh had told his friend what had happened to them, Curt had ushered them quickly into his restaurant.

Despite their best efforts, Penelope wouldn't respond to them. She simply stared at the candle. Hugh knew she was in shock. He couldn't blame her. He was still taken aback by the evening's events, and he'd known the truth about what was in the world from birth.

Curt poured himself a drink from the aged bourbon as well. "Hugh, all kidding aside, do you think she might be your mate?"

Hugh spun around to stare at his longtime friend. "What? No. Wait. Maybe. Butter rum squash cookies!"

Curt held back his laughter—barely. "Buster told me about the drink Polly sent you. I'd heard she has money riding on our bet. Looks like she made sure you couldn't lose."

"He's a giant dog," Penelope said softly, but loud enough for both Curt and Hugh to pick up on with their supernatural hearing. While Hugh wasn't thrilled to be called a dog rather than a wolf, he was happy to hear Penelope speaking at all.

Curt grinned. "You really should explain the difference between wolves and dogs to your mate."

My mate?

Hugh paled. Could Penelope really be his? That one person created just for him? She was a Messing. What were the odds a Messing and a Lupine would be destined for one another? They'd been on opposite sides of the fence since the dawn of time.

Hugh thought about the strange pull to Penelope. About how it had always been there to some degree, even when they were young. He thought about the fierce need he possessed to protect her. About how he'd reacted to seeing her laughing with Curt, and gifting him smiles that should have been reserved for Hugh. He thought about the way he craved her kisses, her touch. About the way he'd thought of little else other than her all day since, she'd struck him with her car. He thought about how he'd struggled more than once around her with his shifter side.

As all the pieces fell into place, Curt's words began to make sense.

Curt quietly watched him as if he were waiting for it all to sink in. When it did, Hugh grabbed the glass of whiskey and drank it down in one gulp. It burned, but so did the knowledge that he'd not only met his mate, but she was from a family that had a history of killing *his* family. One that had rumored ties to his mother's death.

Could he live with that knowledge? Could he love Penelope as fate had decided he should?

Another sobering thought hit him: he was already falling in love with the quirky, quick-witted woman. If he was being truthful with himself, he'd always been in love with her to some degree, even from a young age. He didn't chase after every car leaving Everlasting, but he had when her grandparents took her from town twenty years ago.

The truth that he wasn't a playboy and really did want a future with the woman who wore puppy dog sweaters crashed into him.

"Poodles with umbrellas!" he shouted, only serving to make Curt laugh.

"You're totally fearsome now. Some alpha wolf you are," said Curt. "Next you'll be yelling about teddy bears."

Hugh snarled, letting a bit of his wolf side show through. "I wonder if Polly's spell extends to me strangling you?"

Curt laughed more as if he didn't have a care in the world. "Probably not, but this is too good for me to pass up."

"The man turns into an animal," Penelope said, still staring at the lit candle. Her expression was blank, like the words weren't totally computing in her brain as of yet. The smallest of snorts came from her. "All men are dogs, so this really does just confirm it."

Hugh grunted as Curt found more humor in the situation.

Curt lifted his hand high in the air. "Not all men are dogs. I'm a cat."

Penelope didn't so much as blink in their direction. "Sure. Why not? You should have picked a unicorn, not a cat. I'm allergic to those. Or a pony. I always wanted a pony."

"It doesn't work that way, honey," said Hugh, feeling bad for all she was trying to wrap her mind around.

"Unicorns are real," said Curt, partially under his breath. "She has a point. It would be cooler to be a unicorn-shifter than a cat one."

"You're not helping," stressed Hugh.

"I know." Curt flashed his pearly whites.

"When you find your mate, I hope she takes you and gets you fixed," said Hugh. "Or at the very least, declawed."

Curt's eyes widened. "Bite your tongue. I'm nowhere near ready to settle down. And I like all my bits just where they are, thank you very much."

"And you think I was ready to settle down this morning when I woke up?" asked Hugh.

It was Curt's turn to pale. His face was ashen as he swayed in place.

"Yeah, chew on that thought for a while," snapped Hugh.

"Excuse me," said Curt as he hurried into the

back office area, looking as though he might be sick at the idea of finding his mate.

"Chicken!" called Hugh, happy that word had been the one he'd been aiming at. He then turned to face Penelope and realized he was the real chicken in the situation, not Curt. He'd tried to tell himself he was giving her space to process everything she'd seen tonight when in reality, he was avoiding her. Digging deep to find his suddenly cowardly alpha side, he covered the distance to Penelope. "Honey, I know this is a lot to absorb. I wish I could make it easier for you. I'm sorry so much has been sprung on you in such a short period of time."

He was just about to touch her shoulder when someone began pounding on the locked front door. This time of night there shouldn't be anyone down near the docks. At last check, none of the locals who docked boats at his marina were out on the water, and even so, they wouldn't have any reason to be at Curt's restaurant this late at night.

The idea that someone might be there to try to harm Penelope hit him hard, and Hugh had to fight with his wolf side to keep it under wraps while he assessed the situation. "Don't move," he said to Penelope before remembering she'd not so much as budged from the second he'd set her in the chair.

Hugh took a few steps in the direction of the

front door and then spotted Wilber Messing through the glass.

"Boy, you've got one second to get your backside over here and open this door, or I'll break it down and have your hide on my wall," said the older man, his threat real. "I might even mount your head above my fireplace."

Curt rushed out from the back area of the restaurant, his eyes wide. "Oh crap. He looks ticked."

"Yeah," said Hugh, marching for the door, his fear of Wilber gone. With what he'd been through so far today, a hunter really didn't rank high on his worry list. He opened the door wide and folded his arms over his chest, his gaze firm and on Wilber. "Calm down. She's had a rough night, and she's scared enough as it is. Seeing us go at it won't help her any."

Wilber grinned slightly, but the smile never reached his eyes. "I wondered when you'd find your spine around me, Lupine."

Hugh nearly took offense. His pride was low on his list of concerns at the moment. Penelope was his main worry. Right now, she needed reassurance, not Hugh wrestling with her grandfather. "Come on in. Maybe you can get her to snap out of her shocked state. We can't."

Curt put his hands up and took a giant step

back. "I'm innocent in this. Don't make a rug out of me."

"Relax," said Wilber, hurrying past Curt on his way to Penelope. "I already know what happened. My crystal balls showed me. You okay? What I saw wasn't pretty, and for a minute I didn't think you'd make it."

Hugh was surprised the man cared enough to bother asking. He wasn't that taken aback by the crystal ball comment. Everlasting was full of weird things, and Wilber was known to collect and oversee them. It made sense the man would be in possession of crystal balls. "I'm fine. Thanks to your granddaughter. Her quick thinking saved my life."

"She's a good girl," said Wilber, heading right for her. He knelt near Penelope and put a hand on her thigh lightly. "Hey, sweetheart, you had one heck of an eventful evening, didn't you?"

She faced him, her expression blank. "I saw a ghost in boxers, got accused of murder, hit a guy with my car, had the best date ever that suddenly turned into a scene from the movie *Jaws*. It's been an eventful *day*, Grandpa."

The best date ever?

She'd enjoyed herself? At least up until the attack?

Wilber sighed. "I know, sweetheart. I'm sorry. Everlasting tends to never have a dull moment. Seems as though it had some catching up to do with you since you were gone so long. I suspect things will level out soon enough."

She put her hand over her grandfather's. "Hugh was so worried about me during it all. I could sense it. I just knew he was thinking of me, not of the fact he was about to drown. I could feel it deep down, and for a second, I could have sworn that I heard his panic in my head. He didn't care about his life. He was only worried about me. I wasn't the one about to be eaten by a Kraken. He was."

She'd sensed that? How?

Curt covered his mouth partially and did a rather poor job of whispering, "Yeah, in *no way* is she your mate."

Wilber's gaze snapped up and landed on Hugh. He then regarded his granddaughter and Hugh once more before sighing. "I really wish you weren't the one fate brought her back to Everlasting for. I was hoping it was Curt."

"Gee, thanks," said Hugh, folding his arms over his chest. Wrestling with the man sounded better and better. "Love you too, Gramps."

Wilber narrowed his gaze on him.

Curt eased his way closer to Penelope and Wilber. Within seconds, Penelope was sneezing nonstop.

Hugh snorted. "She's allergic to you, Curt."

Penelope looked up, her eyes finding Curt. Hugh assumed she'd burst into tears. She didn't.

Instead, she started to laugh—hard. "Oh my stars, *I am* allergic to you. You really are a cat-shifter, aren't you?"

"Guilty," said Curt with a soft smile. "Lion-shifter."

Penelope touched her grandfather's arm lightly. "Grandpa, the stories you used to tell me when I was little…"

Wilber nodded, leaning in toward his granddaughter. "Weren't just stories. I know, sweetheart. I never knew how to fully get the truth of it all across to you. Your father wasn't big on me telling you any of it. He seemed to think he could raise you here, free from the taint of our family's long history."

"Grandpa, did my parents really die in an automobile accident?" asked Penelope, sounding so young and vulnerable that it broke Hugh's heart.

"No," said Wilber, his voice tight. "They stood up for the supernaturals here and in the end, outside forces didn't much like that. They stepped in and put a stop to it."

Hugh drew in a deep breath. Penelope's parents had died because they'd protected the supernaturals in Everlasting?

Wilber glanced up and met Hugh's gaze. "When my daughter-in-law took a stand against my extended family and what they did to your family, it was the line in the sand. My son stood by her choice. I didn't understand it fully then, but I do now. It was the right thing to do."

Penelope remained strangely calm. "I don't want anything to happen to anyone in Everlasting either. Does that mean a target is on me now too?"

Growling, Hugh nearly lunged forward in protest, but Curt caught him, obviously sensing the pending outburst.

"Take a deep breath, Lupine," warned Curt.

"Anyone tries to hurt my woman, and I'll shove my dandelions up their watermelon," snarled Hugh.

Curt laughed. "Gee, that will show them."

Wilber looked confused but focused his attention on his granddaughter. "Sweetheart, the faction of my family that hurt your parents have been dealt with accordingly. While they are no longer a threat, there are others out there who share their opinions. They won't be happy to hear a natural-born hunter and a wolf-shifter are together. They may try to interfere. You should know that you'll have me at your back, and I'm guessing that heathen you seem to like so much will also be there to protect you."

"Without a doubt," said Hugh.

Curt nodded. "I will too. And I know everyone she's met here so far would stand behind her as well. Plus, from what I was told by Hugh, Penelope is fierce when need be."

Pride shone on Wilber's face. "She was born

with the gifts of my kind. They're in there. She just needs practice."

"We'll work with her every day," said Hugh quickly.

Penelope's shoulders slumped. "I could never hunt anything or anyone. That isn't me. None of this is me."

Dark shadows appeared around Wilber's eyes. "You're going to leave Everlasting now, aren't you? This scared you away, didn't it?"

Hugh's throat closed quickly as worry that Penelope would leave him hit him hard. "No!"

All eyes went to him.

With a cough, he cleared his throat. "She can't go."

Wilber quirked a brow. "And why might that be?"

The man was going to make Hugh say it out loud. With a grumble, Hugh spoke. "Because she's my mate."

Curt clapped quickly and then stopped just as fast. "Champagne is probably out of the question?"

The look Wilber gave Curt shut the man right up.

Penelope turned to face Hugh. Her expression was blank, and he knew she was still in shock. "I don't know what that means. Are you saying I'm your friend? We can be friends and not be in the same town, Lupine."

He hid a smile at her sass that managed to poke through even in her state of shock. She'd been hit with a lot in one day. It could make anyone question everything. She was handling it all better than most would.

Better than he would if he were in her shoes.

He eased up alongside her and knelt, mirroring Wilber but on Penelope's other side. He touched her arm gently. "Honey, it means so much more than that."

Her brow crinkled. "So, you don't think I'm going to really poison you now?"

He snorted. "Well, I know me, so I'm guessing at some point in our life you will totally give it a try."

"Just give him chocolate," added Curt from the peanut gallery. "It doesn't do good things for dogs."

"Not helping here, Curt," stressed Hugh.

Wilber grinned from ear to ear. "Oh, I think he's helping a ton. Carry on."

"Onions and grapes would do the trick too," offered Curt, laughing as he did.

"Tell me again why we're friends," said Hugh, staying close to Penelope.

Curt chuckled. "Because Sigmund and I are the only two people dumb enough to put up with you."

"He has you there, Lupine," said Wilber.

Penelope locked gazes with Hugh. "I don't mind putting up with you. Jolene told me you'd be difficult, but that your bark was worse than your bite. She said she wouldn't have thought to pair me with you, but she's not been wrong before about who goes with who around here."

Hugh and Wilber stared at each other, their expressions the same—shocked. Jolene's matchmaking skills had never once been wrong. And if she said Penelope and Hugh were a match, that meant he was right; she was his mate.

The odds of a Messing and a Lupine being a mated pair just became a heck of a lot higher.

Hugh cleared his throat. "W-what?"

Wilber scowled. "You heard the girl. As much as I dislike you, you foul-mouthed heathen, Jolene has never been wrong. And the crystal balls showed me what my granddaughter did to get you out of that water and away from that creature. She tapped into a side of herself she's always denied. She pulled on the hunter in her bloodline to save you, a shifter. Guess times certainly are a changin'."

"I'd say so," added Curt.

Hugh cast his friend a hard look.

Curt winked. "Call me a poodle with an umbrella. I like that one best."

"What's he going on about?" asked Wilber.

Hugh sighed. "Did you hear about the bet he and I made?"

"The one that says you can't go a month without saying something foul?" asked Wilber.

"Yeah, that one."

Wilber nodded.

"Polly took it upon herself to make sure I couldn't lose."

Wilber's eyes widened. "I almost feel sorry for you. She tried to help me find true love once, and my car kept breaking down for three straight months. I'm pretty sure Jolene thought I was sabotaging the darn thing myself just to see her."

Penelope leaned in toward Hugh, and he wrapped an arm around her as she looked at her grandfather. "She cares for you, Grandpa. A lot."

"Who? Polly? She's got a thing for old Cornelius."

"The ghost in the boxers?" asked Penelope.

Wilber groaned. "Yeah, that old goat."

Penelope shook her head. "I wasn't talking about Polly. I was talking about Jolene. She's got a thing for you. I think you're the love that got away from her. Her chance at happiness."

Wilber drew up short.

Penelope stood slowly, and Hugh did as well. She turned into his arms, and he pulled her close, hugging her tight and rocking their bodies. He kissed her forehead lightly. "Thanks for saving my life."

"Least I could do since I ran you over with my car," she said.

"That was hardly a car," he returned, knowing it would make her smile. He wasn't disappointed.

Wilber gave him the side-eye. "Penelope, we should get you home so you can rest."

As Penelope drew back from Hugh, he instantly felt the loss of her. Worry tugged at him. He didn't want to let her out of his sight. Something had attacked them tonight, and he didn't want to risk anything else happening to her.

Curt spoke up. "Should we put a call into the sheriff about what happened out by the cliffs?"

"We should tell Deputy March," said Penelope. "That thing that attacked us might be what killed those men."

Wilber cringed and glanced away quickly as lines of strain appeared on his face. He was hiding something.

Hugh thought about the number of times he'd tried to reach Deputy March throughout the day. And then he thought about Wilber's disappearing act. "Messing, you wouldn't happen to know where Jake is, would you?"

"Why would Grandpa know where Deputy March is?" questioned Penelope.

Hugh kept his gaze fixed on the older man. Penelope may still think he was innocent, but Hugh knew better. "Gee, I don't know why. Could be because Jake liked you for the murders and your grandfather would do anything to protect you."

She went to her grandfather's side. "Tell them that isn't true."

He cleared his throat. "Sweetheart, March was going to create a whole lot of problems for you. I simply made sure he was out of the way while I tried to figure out what really happened to those men."

"Oh my stars, you killed Deputy March?" Penelope shook her head. "Grandpa!"

Wilber huffed. "I didn't kill him. I just tied him up in one of my tucked-away safe houses, just outside of town. I left a television on for him. He's fine."

Curt laughed.

Hugh shot him a nasty look. "How is Wilber tying up Jake funny?"

"How is it not?" countered Curt.

Wilber looked to Curt. "You can come out with me while I untie him. Then you can tell him what happened."

"That would be better coming from Hugh. He was there," said Curt. "I can get Penelope back to your house."

Hugh didn't want to leave Penelope, but he trusted Curt with his life. Now he'd need to trust him with his mate's life. "Stay there until we get back. I don't want her alone right now. Not until we know more about what is going on."

"One hair on my granddaughter's head gets so

much as out of place, and I'll make you into that rug you were so afraid of," warned Wilber.

Curt gulped.

Penelope snorted. "Enough, Grandpa. Stop scaring the poor man, and go release Deputy March. No more tying people up and no making rugs out of anyone."

Wilber grumbled as he headed for the door.

Hugh followed, laughing as he did.

Chapter Eighteen

As Hugh pulled his diesel pickup truck to a stop outside of an old, rundown cabin in the woods on the outskirts of town, he couldn't help but look at Wilber. The man hadn't said much since Hugh had insisted on driving to the location where Wilber was holding Jake. For a brief, tension-filled moment at the start of it all, Wilber had refused to divulge the location he was holding Jake. It wasn't until after Hugh pointed out Penelope would be furious with him that Wilber conceded and grumbled the address.

Hugh hadn't been out on these back roads in years and didn't think they were traveled on anymore. The roads weren't in the best shape and many splintered off into unofficial roads that weren't paved; such was the case with the one they were on now. Thankfully, the storms that had happened closer to town, near the shoreline, hadn't seemed to dump much rain farther inland. Hugh wasn't sure he'd have made it down the path had it been muddy.

The cabin, while standing, looked abandoned. Its windows and front door were boarded up. There were a number of old "no trespassing" signs posted on the edge of the property, near the dirt road. A hand-painted sign was nailed to a tree. It read "Trespassers Won't Be Seen Again."

Hugh nodded to the sign. "That your handiwork?"

That earned him a smile from the older man. "Yes. Like it?"

"You're twisted."

"Thanks," said Wilber, his chest puffing out slightly with pride.

Hugh knew without a shadow of a doubt that Penelope was his mate. That meant Wilber would be family to him. The idea of it nearly made Hugh groan in frustration.

"Penelope sees you as a sweet, gentle old man," said Hugh. "When are you going to tell her that you're anything but?"

Wilber stared forward. "I didn't kill March. He shouldn't have a bruise on him. I was careful with him."

"Because he's human and hunters live by a code to protect them at all costs," said Hugh.

Wilber turned to face him. "March is anything but human. I'm surprised you can't smell that on him. Your kind are good with scents."

Hugh jerked. Jake was a supernatural? No. He couldn't be. Hugh would have sensed it. He'd have smelled it on him. Wilber was right. Shifters had an amazing ability to pick up scents, even days old. Surely he'd have known if Jake was really something more than human.

Wilber opened the truck door and jumped out with a speed and grace a man his age shouldn't still have. Cutting the engine, Hugh took a deep breath, drawing in the scents around him, concerned this might be a trap. He wanted to trust Wilber because of Penelope, but he was smarter than that. When he caught a whiff of Jake's scent, he relaxed. The faint sound of muffled curses found his sensitive ears, and he knew then Jake was not only still alive, but he was also mad.

Hugh couldn't blame him.

He'd be mad too. Though with Polly's potion he'd probably start shouting about cats in bikinis or something, so voicing his anger was pointless and humiliating. He followed quickly behind Wilber, catching up to him with ease. They went around the back of the old cabin, around a large woodpile, and to a back porch. The steps were nearly rotted through, so the men walked on the edges of them.

Wilber put a hand out, stopping Hugh in mid-motion. The older man pointed to a series of stakes that were to the side of the railing at the top of the steps. He then motioned in the direction of a tripwire.

"Great, I'm on a mission with Rambo," said Hugh, partially under his breath.

With a shrug, Wilber stepped over the tripwire. "I didn't need to tell you about it."

"I'm guessing your granddaughter wouldn't be too happy with you if you staked me."

"You'd have lived. Sure, you'd be sore for a few days, but stakes don't kill shifters," said Wilber as he went for the back door. He opened it, and Hugh entered behind him.

When Hugh spotted Jake tied to a chair, a gag in his mouth and the television on the Home Shopping Network, he found himself laughing as well.

Jake scooted the chair around and then fell onto his side. He looked up at Hugh and then to Wilber. Anger flashed in the deputy's eyes. Snarling, he said something that was muffled by the gag in his mouth. The fire in the man's dark gaze said everything he was unable to verbalize.

Hugh put up his hands. "Relax, we come in peace, and we're here to spring you."

Wilber went to Jake, bent and undid the gag.

Jake let out of a line of obscenities that made Hugh feel like an amateur. As Wilber undid the ropes binding Jake's hands, Jake made a move to grab the man.

Wilber dodged Jake's grasp and then undid the man's feet, dodging yet another strike. It looked like the older man was toying with the younger one. Knowing the history of the hunters, Hugh had no doubt that was the case.

"If you're finished playing with him," stressed Hugh to Wilber.

Sighing, Wilber yanked Jake to his feet and dusted off the man's uniform shirt. "See. Right as rain. Not a scratch on him."

"You're a regular Boy Scout," injected Hugh sarcastically.

Jake glared at Wilber.

Hugh stepped forward. "I know you're upset with him. You have every right to be, but hear me out for a minute."

Jake eyed him. "I'm past upset. I'm furious."

"Noted," said Hugh.

"The entire Messing family is full of criminals. He's proven my point," snapped Jake.

Hugh sighed. "Jake, Penelope didn't kill those men. I think you already know that. Tonight, I took her out on one of my sailboats to the area near the cliff where the bodies were found. While we were there, we were attacked by a kraken."

Jake didn't bother to hide his shock. "I'm sorry, but what did you say attacked you?"

"A kraken," repeated Hugh.

"Those aren't real," returned Jake, giving Wilber a threatening look.

"Yeah, well most would argue that a centaur couldn't be real, let alone running around town, working as a deputy, and posing for pictures in a calendar. They'd be wrong, wouldn't they, Deputy March?"

Hugh gasped. Jake was a centaur?

Centaurs were real too?

Suddenly, he got a pretty good idea of what Penelope must feel like, having so much thrown at her that seemed impossible.

Jake rubbed his wrists and grunted in Wilber's direction. "I don't like you."

"Get in line, horse-boy," said Wilber.

"Yeah, behind me. Though the man is starting to slowly grow on me," supplied Hugh.

"Like a rash?" asked Jake.

Wilber ignored their comments. "What are we going to do about the kraken? One hasn't been seen around these parts in nearly a hundred years."

"Everlasting has a history of krakens?" asked Hugh, dumbfounded.

"Boy, do you think all those ships years and years ago just up and decided to crash themselves?" Wilber stared at Hugh as if he were a moron.

"I never actually gave much thought to it," confessed Hugh.

"Some sailor you are," mouthed Wilber.

Jake went to the side of the cabin, to an old table that looked as though it was standing only because of the amount of dust on it. He retrieved his gun belt and put it on, glaring at Wilber the entire time. "I should arrest you."

"Go ahead. Won't be my first or last time," said Wilber, holding out his wrists. "Besides, Sheriff Bull adores me. She'll let me out two minutes after you're done processing me in."

"I think the kraken is what killed the men," said Hugh. "It got hold of me and let me tell you, it nearly did me in."

Jake took in a deep breath, looking tired. "The injuries on the men show they were crushed to death. I assumed a hunter did it. They're the only ones around here that I know could do that kind of damage. That was before I found out about the kraken."

Hugh rubbed his chest, remembering all too well what it felt like to have the kraken's tentacle wrapped around him, squeezing the air from his lungs. "Oh, trust me, the kraken is more than capable of that."

Wilber stepped forward. "You do know those two men were from the Collective, right?"

Hugh froze. The Collective was back in Everlasting? They were an organization full of power-hungry zealots who would stop at nothing to get what they wanted. If they were in town that meant Everlasting had a problem.

Jake finished securing his gun belt. "Are you sure?"

"Yes," said Wilber, his tone clipped. "And they aren't the only ones in town."

"Fish sticks!" exclaimed Hugh, drawing amused looks from the other men. He offered a hand gesture that couldn't be mistaken for anything other than what it was.

Jake snorted. "There is the Hugh I know."

"Let's get out of here and try to hunt down this kraken," said Hugh.

"It did us a favor," said Wilber. "It killed two men who would have no doubt done something horrible here in town."

Hugh agreed to a point. "But it attacked Penelope and me. That means innocents could end up hurt. We need to stop it before someone else ends up dead."

"How does one find a kraken?" asked Jake.

Wilber shut off the television. "We go fishing. But not until tomorrow night. They tend to hunt only after the sun has set."

Chapter Nineteen

Penelope entered Witch's Brew and instantly felt at home. Nothing in the small coffee shop matched furniture wise, but that only added to the charm. It was the type of place one would want to come with a book to enjoy a cup of coffee and a good read.

Several people moved past her to the exit and their tables filled quickly with new customers. The place was busy especially with how early it was. Penelope had woken at the crack of dawn to find a note from her grandfather telling her to sleep in and leave the shop closed for the day. He also mentioned he was with Hugh and not to worry.

Of course, that made her worry.

She'd found Buster asleep in another guest room, and she'd left him there to shower and ready herself for the day. Curt had left a note on the kitchen table, letting her know he'd called in Buster to watch over her because he was worried Hugh, Jake, and Wilber would kill themselves if left unattended. He was probably right.

Buster hadn't budged as she'd let herself out of the house. There was no way she could stay confined to her grandfather's home after learning that things that went bump in the night were not only real, but able to nearly sink a boat.

No. She needed to be out and about.

She was too curious to do nothing, and if she was right, Polly would be able to shed more light on it all. There was an older woman behind the counter, wearing an apron that said "Kiss the Witch, I'm not Irish." Though the woman was wearing a large shamrock necklace in direct contradiction to her apron. Her unnaturally red hair was pulled up in a tight bun. Penelope wasn't certain, but the woman's earrings looked to be dice. Nothing about the woman's outfit made sense, but then again, Penelope's chosen attire rarely fit together either.

Case in point, Penelope was currently in a red baby doll cotton dress that had small black antique bicycles printed on it. She wore it with a pair of black tights and thigh-high black leather boots that had a two-inch heel. Her hair was pulled into a high ponytail and she had on a medium-gray sweater duster.

The woman glanced up briefly, smiled, and then

looked at something on the floor behind the counter. "Herman, behave yourself."

Wondering what was happening, Penelope moved closer to the counter and leaned. There, on the floor, was an inflated, small baby pool with a lobster in it. The thing actually appeared to be looking up at the redheaded woman. It snapped its claw a few times in what seemed like protest.

The redhead scowled. "Enough of that or I'll get the rubber bands out. I know how you hate those."

Without a doubt, the redhead had to be the woman Penelope was searching for. "Polly?"

The redhead stared up at her and smiled wide. "Penelope! I wondered when you'd stop by. I have your order ready."

"My order?" asked Penelope. She hadn't ordered anything. And how did the woman know her name?

Polly stepped away from the counter and returned with a to-go box. She handed it to Penelope. "Cranberry scones and cheesecake."

Stunned, Penelope just stood there. "Did my grandfather call this in?"

Polly glanced down at the lobster. "One more outburst like that and it's back to the tank with you, young man."

"Um, excuse me," Penelope said, unsure if she should interrupt the woman who was having a one-sided argument with a lobster. Was this the same woman everyone had talked about? No one mentioned she talked to lobsters.

"Yes?" asked Polly. "Did you want me to include cranberry toppings for the cheesecake? You should know, Hugh doesn't like them. He'll like it plain better. Trust me."

Confused, Penelope stood there with a blank expression on her face.

Polly grinned. "Oh, and don't tell Hugh the scones and cheesecake are from me."

Penelope snapped out of her stupor. "Because he'll get fleas again?"

Tsking, Polly shook her head. "I didn't intend for that to happen. In my defense, how was I to know the area had an uptick in fleas during that time? I can hardly be blamed for that." She leaned closer to the counter and lowered her voice. "If anyone asks, I had nothing to do with the locust incident last year."

"Got it. You're innocent in that respect," said Penelope as she began to follow along with the woman's strange string of logic. She found it endearing and Polly adorable.

With a wink, Polly pushed the to-go box at Penelope. "You're a good star fruit."

Star fruit?

The woman sounded like Hugh.

Penelope laughed softly. "Thank you."

"Anytime."

Petey entered the coffee shop and stopped just inside the door. He held a wadded-up newspaper in one arm and with his free hand he smoothed his unruly hair to one side. It instantly poked back up as if it had never been touched. He had on a pair of jean overalls and a green plaid shirt. He rounded off his look with a pair of fishing boots.

When he spotted Penelope, he smiled wide. "How was your romantic evening? You didn't eat the fish sticks, did you?"

She took a deep breath. "It was different. By chance have you talked to Hugh yet?"

"No. His main fishing charter boat was gone when I got up. I'm taking a group of tourists out later, and hadn't noticed another group on the books for this morning," said Petey. He glanced forward and then cleared his throat before handing the newspaper to Penelope.

She took it—and instantly regretted the decision. It smelled horrible. "What is in this?"

"The catch of the day. I gotta give it to my love muffin before Anna gets back or she'll yell at me again," said Petey.

Penelope followed his gaze to find Polly there, taking a tray of fresh-baked muffins from the oven.

Petey reached into his back pocket and pulled out a fifth of whiskey. He opened it and dabbed some on his fingertips before rubbing it on his face as if it were aftershave.

Gasping, Penelope shook her head, unable to believe what she was seeing. "Petey, what are you doing?"

"I want to smell good for Polly, my goddess, my sweet Venus, the bread to my butter, the bait to my hook," he said proudly.

She sighed. "Oh, Petey, that isn't the way to do it."

"It's not?" he asked, looking confused.

Penelope glanced up to see Polly busy helping other customers. "No. I can help you if you want. We should also talk about what happened last night."

He grunted. "What did Hugh screw up this time? Did you hit him with a boat instead of a car? He probably deserved it."

"It involved a kraken," said Penelope, doing her best to keep her voice down.

"A kraken!" shouted Petey, drawing the attention of other patrons of the coffee shop.

Polly looked up, holding a coffeepot, her eyes wide. "Oh, not again."

A heavily tattooed woman came rushing in, nearly knocking the wadded newspaper that smelled like death from Penelope's hands.

The woman paused. "Sorry." She looked toward

Polly. "I'm sorry I'm late. Thanks for covering for me."

"I love helping, Marcy," said Polly, refilling a man's coffee. "Think nothing of it. Did you finish all the deliveries?"

"I did. Took me longer than normal because several tourists got into a fender bender over on Main Street." Marcy moved behind the counter and put on an apron. She glanced at the tray of muffins Polly had pulled from the oven and frowned. "Tell me you weren't baking again, Polly."

Polly pointed at Penelope. "She did it! Ask Herman, he'll back me up."

Marcy snorted. "Okay, but if Anna asks I'm going to lie."

Polly grinned. "Good call."

A man in a tracksuit walked up to the counter and ordered a muffin. Marcy went to grab one of the freshly baked ones but Polly was there in an instant, slapping the woman's hand lightly. "That isn't for him." She pulled two raisin cookies with two large dates on top from the display case and handed them to the man. "Here."

He looked at them as if they might bite. "I want a blueberry muffin."

"No, you don't. You want this. It will get you regular and back on track in no time," said Polly with a wide smile.

The man grunted, but paid for his cookies and left quickly.

"Poor Jerry. He's always cranky when he's bound up. Plus, I added a little something special to help with his hair loss."

Marcy let out a long breath. "Great. Jerry will be a yeti by tomorrow morning."

Polly grinned. "Well, that would solve his thinning hair problem."

Penelope couldn't help but fall in love with the woman. In some ways, it was like looking into the future and seeing herself. "Polly, can I have a minute of your time?"

"You can have her for the day," added Marcy.

Polly gave the woman a sharp look. "Stop trying to give me away."

"I'll take you, Polly," said Petey sweetly.

"I know," returned Polly. She walked around the counter to Penelope and took the newspaper. She looked to Petey. "Are you giving other women the catch of the day now?"

Petey blushed. "I'd never do that."

Polly set the wad on the counter with a thud.

Marcy groaned at the sight of it. "Anna will not be happy."

"When is she ever?" asked Polly. Her attention returned to Penelope. In an instant, the redheaded woman had her finger in the air, indicating that Penelope was to wait a moment, and she was rushing off. She vanished behind a curtain. Above it, there was a sign announcing Polly's Perfectly Magical Mystical Wondrous World of Wonders.

"Um, Wondrous Wonders?" asked Penelope as Marcy walked by.

Marcy slowed her pace. "You should have heard her first choice. I'm pretty sure it was like a hundred words, sixty of which were versions of the word 'wonder.'"

Everlasting was a very strange town indeed.

Penelope lifted the box of baked goods Polly had left on the counter for her and looked to Marcy. "How much do I owe you for this?"

Marcy shook her head. "Nothing."

"I have to pay *something*," stressed Penelope.

"Trust me. Anna would have my head if I charged for anything Polly made."

"Will Anna be back soon? I was hoping to talk to her and Polly," said Penelope, hoping the women could shed more light on all she'd learned.

Marcy laughed. "I'm pretty sure she's on a date. I doubt she's realized that yet though." With that, Marcy hurried off with a pot of coffee and went around to each table, topping off patrons' cups.

Polly returned from behind the curtain, looking like the cat that ate the canary. She had a necklace made of black cord with a white crystal on the end of it. She held it out as she covered the distance to

Penelope and then handed it to her. "Here. This is for you."

"It's beautiful. How much?" she asked.

Polly pursed her lips. "Nothing. It decided it wanted to live with you. Who am I to charge for that?"

"I can't take that," said Penelope. "Thank you though."

"Nonsense. It's supposed to be with you," said Polly. "Trust me. I know these things. Now, you go on out of here and if I can make a suggestion."

"Of course."

"Take the long way down to the marina," said Polly with a wink as she walked off, leaving Petey staring after her with a look of longing on his face.

Penelope couldn't help but feel bad for the man. It was evident he was smitten with Polly, but didn't have a clue as to how to romance a woman. Penelope offered a warm smile to Petey. "Mind walking me to the docks? I'd like to see if Hugh is back."

"I'd be honored to be your escort, my lady," he said, holding his arm out.

"Can we take the long way?" asked Penelope, slipping the necklace on and then taking hold of the box of goodies.

"Of course."

Chapter Twenty

"Please let me kill him," said Jake to Hugh about Wilber.

Wilber held a harpoon gun and gave Jake a look that begged the man to try.

Curt sat in a chair on the deck, his feet propped on the side of the fishing boat. "They're like taking small children places, aren't they?"

Hugh had to agree. Jake and Wilber had been taking verbal jabs at one another since they'd started their hunting expedition. As the hours ticked on with not so much as a hint of the sea creature, tensions had begun to mount among the crew.

If they didn't find the kraken soon, there was a high likelihood there would be mutiny onboard. His luck, they'd toss him overboard. That was how his week was going. And if they did toss him over, the kraken would make a sudden daylight appearance and eat him.

Yep.

Sounded about right.

"We're not going to find it," said Curt, opening a beer. He'd shown up on the docks with a cooler of beer and snacks, claiming he wanted to lend a hand in the hunt. Hugh suspected Curt's sudden arrival had more to do with him worrying Hugh would attack Wilber or vice versa. After Curt had assured Hugh that he'd left Penelope in good hands, they'd headed out. It wasn't until they were nearly to the cliffs that Curt confessed those good hands actually belonged to Buster, not Sigmund, as Curt had led Hugh to believe.

It had taken both Jake and Wilber to pull Hugh off Curt. Over the course of the night, cooler heads had prevailed.

"Wil said it likes to hunt at night," added Curt. "The sun has been up for hours. I vote we try again tonight, and we can bring pizza out with us. We're out of chips and pretzels now."

"For a guy who owns a fancy restaurant you brought cheap chips," said Jake.

"Expensive beer though," added Curt with a grin. "Hey, I'm bored. Let's put boxing gloves on Wil and Jake and see who can win in a fight. My money is on the old guy."

"Thanks. I knew I liked you better than Hugh

for a reason." Wilber grinned and for a brief moment Hugh wondered about the man's true age.

Shifters tended to live longer than most, and aged at a slower rate than humans and many other supernaturals. He didn't know much about hunters other than they were technically more than human. How much more, he wasn't sure. He did know they were strong and fast, as proven by Penelope yanking him over the edge of the boat with one hand and sending him across the deck.

"Wil, how do you know so much about hunting kraken?" questioned Hugh. "Do your hunter books talk about them?"

"They do," answered Wilber, looking off into the distance. "But I've hunted them before in my life. There was one that terrorized the waters off Everlasting a while back."

"You mean a century ago," said Hugh.

"Yes. About that." Wilber stiffened and then glanced at Hugh.

"How old are you? For real?" Hugh needed to know. The idea that he'd age slower than Penelope terrified him. He didn't want to think about seeing her grow old and die. He wanted to grow old with her.

Curt and Jake looked in Wilber's direction. Clearly they were curious as well.

Wilber clicked his tongue on his inner cheek. "I'm pushing two hundred."

"Ha, Jake, you got your butt handed to you by a two-hundred-year-old man," teased Curt.

Jake ran a hand through his hair. "I'm nearly five hundred."

Curt gulped and glanced at Hugh. "We're like babies here."

Hugh spoke. "Jake, why didn't you ever tell us what you are? Why did I have to learn about it from Wilber—and how did *he* know?"

Jake shrugged. "No clue how he figured it out. I haven't told anyone since I came to Everlasting. It's not something I spread around. I've got a long history and most of it isn't pretty. It was best I find a spot where I could blend in and sort of fade away into obscurity."

"I can feel what a supernatural is when I'm near them. Long ago, hunters used to be given crystals that would glow when we were close to what we were to be hunting," offered Wilber freely. "My granddaughter will develop the ability to sense supernaturals too. She'll age slowly from this point forward. I leveled off around twenty-five and then basically aged at a snail's pace since then."

"How old does Penelope think you are?" questioned Hugh.

"She thinks I'm in my early seventies."

"Won't she be in for a surprise," joked Curt. "Sweetheart, soon you'll be able to sense all the wacky things around you and, oh, by the way, you've stopped aging."

Jake laughed. "That was basically how I found out what I was."

Hugh stared out at the calm ocean. "Curt is right. We should head in. I need to check on Penelope. Buster better have done his job or Everlasting will be one were-rat short by the end of the day.

"Going to shove your sunflower up his whoops-a-daisy?" asked Curt before sipping his beer.

Hugh growled.

Jake and Wilber laughed.

"Polly really gave you a drink that is keeping you from cursing?" asked Jake.

With a sigh, Hugh nodded. "Yes."

"When does it wear off?" questioned Jake as he helped himself to a beer from the cooler and then sat on the edge of the boat.

Hugh hadn't thought of the length of the spell. He'd been too stuck on how ridiculous he sounded whenever he was mad. As he realized it might very well be forever, a line of what should have been curses burst free from him.

Six references to peanut butter and jelly sandwiches with bananas on top later and the men on the boat were laughing to the point they teared up. Even Hugh had to admit it was funny, even though he was the butt of the joke.

"This means you lose the bet," said Jake to Curt.

"You're going to have to donate five grand to the middle school fund."

Curt shrugged. "Worth it to hear this. Plus, it's a tax deduction. Why do you think I sponsor softball teams around town and paid for the playground equipment at the park to be updated?"

"Uh, because it's the right thing to do," offered Jake, his voice even.

Hugh laughed at that one. "It's like you don't even know Curt at all."

"He's not so bad," added Wilber, joining the men in having a beer.

Hugh refrained from taking one. He was the one captaining the boat. Drinking and boating didn't mix. He'd seen too many accidents and lives lost to ever drink while he was the one charged with driving the boat.

He wanted to find the creature that had attacked them and make sure it couldn't hurt anyone else. Everlasting had a longstanding way of sweeping supernatural incidents under the rug, but they'd only be able to cover so long if tourists started being eaten by a giant sea monster.

There really was rarely a dull day in Everlasting.

"Curt told me that you think Penelope is your mate," said Jake, drinking more of his beer.

Wilber grunted and then gave Hugh a look that said he was looking for a reason to end him. What else was new?

Hugh smiled sweetly and batted his eyes. "Get used to me, Wilber. I'm about to be family. I'm going to convince your granddaughter to marry me and then you'll be Gramps to me. Let's hug it out now."

As the words left his mouth, Jake choked on his beer and nearly fell overboard. Wilber's quick reflexes kept the man on the boat—just barely. Jake shrugged the older man off. "I'd thank you, but you tied me to a chair for a day."

"I left the television on for you," protested Wilber. "Stop making it out like it was horrible. I didn't skin you or anything. You were entertained all day."

"With a channel that features fake diamonds and must-own cooling appliances." Jake looked to Curt. "Did you know a lot of people will pay for anything? I didn't. Humans are really weird."

Curt lifted his beer. "I'll drink to that."

Wilber raised his beer as well. "They are pretty strange. Speaking of humans, anyone want to take a car ride to Chicago and help me break a guy's legs?"

Understanding what man Wilber wanted to hurt, Hugh raised his hand. "I'm in. So in!"

Wilber snorted. "Thought you might be."

"Who are we going to rough up?" asked Curt.

"I'm going to pretend this conversation isn't happening, seeing as how it's illegal and all," Jake said, drinking more of his beer. "But I'm in if you need me."

"We'd be going for my granddaughter's ex. He broke her heart." Wilber shook his head. "I knew he wasn't good enough for her. He makes Hugh look like a great choice."

"Thanks. I think," replied Hugh as he turned the boat around and headed back in the direction of the marina. If Buster wasn't on sentry duty, keeping Penelope safe, the were-rat would really have to worry about Hugh snacking on him.

"Let's get back to you wanting to marry Penelope," said Curt, an amused look on his face. He reached for a nearly empty bag of chips, propped against the leg of his chair. "How does she feel about this?"

"Uh, haven't had a chance to bring it up with her," admitted Hugh. The back of his neck heated as concern over her reaction came over him. What if she didn't feel the same way for him that he felt for her? What if she left and headed back to Chicago?

"He looks like he's about to puke," said Jake with a snort.

"I know him well," interjected Curt, shoving a handful of tiny, broken bits of chips into his mouth. "Right about now, he's freaking out that she might not want him and that she'll run back to Chicago, leaving him here—alone."

Curt really did know him. Hugh wasn't sure how he felt about that. He glanced away and pretended to be totally focused on the water ahead.

"She'll stay," said Wilber evenly. "It was shown to me."

"In your crystal balls?" asked Curt.

Nodding, Wilber look at Hugh. "They gave me a glimpse of Penelope here in Everlasting, expecting a baby, happy and with a wedding band on her finger. It didn't show me the man with her fully, but I understand that man is you."

Hugh clutched the wheel. He really would end up with Penelope and they'd have a family? Dare he hope? Two days ago, he'd have never dreamt of wanting a family and a future with any woman. Now it was all he wanted.

"Can I look at your crystal ball collection?" asked Curt, eating more chip leftovers. "I want to know the lottery numbers."

"Stuff a strawberry in it, Warrick," said Hugh, making everyone laugh.

Chapter Twenty-One

"And over there is Polly's place," said Petey, pointing to a house just down a bit on the small side street that he and Penelope were walking on.

Penelope did a double take when she spotted the small home that had an army of garden gnomes in the yard. There were large rock sculptures that didn't exactly look natural set throughout the front lawn, with gnomes positioned to look as though they were peeking out. There were birdbaths, small wooden houses on the ends of long poles, and lights strung about. Penelope couldn't be certain but the lawn itself looked to be artificial, like the fake cut plastic that is supposed to look like grass but falls miserably short. It was nearly impossible to see the porch due to the overwhelming number of vines growing over it.

"Thing of beauty, isn't it?" asked Petey.

"It's something all right. Is it painted pink?" she asked, catching a small glimpse through the mass of vines.

"Six different shades. I helped her paint it. It's so Polly." Petey smiled wide.

"It's, erm, lovely." It looked a lot like a bottle of the pink liquid over-the-counter medicine that provided stomach relief had been thrown all over the place uncontrollably. She'd never seen anything quite like it.

She and Petey continued to walk in the direction of the docks. As Polly had suggested, they took the longer way, at least according to Petey. Since Penelope didn't know her way around Everlasting, she wasn't sure where they were going. She merely followed next to the man as he pointed out various residents' homes.

They rounded the corner and nearly walked directly into Sigmund, who was walking and reading a book at the same time. The man had a sexy nerd vibe going for him. He also looked to have been mugged recently.

Gasping, she drew to a stop. "What happened to you?"

His sweater sleeves were pushed up, giving everyone a full view of bandages that covered both forearms. He had another bandage on his neck and his right eye showed traces of bruises.

Petey whistled low and through his teeth (what teeth he had). "Hate to see the other guy."

Sigmund lowered his book and snorted. "I wish the story was that thrilling. Unfortunately, I'm not exactly sure what happened to me. I went home early last night because my allergies were acting up. I took more meds and then headed to bed. Woke up this morning on my front lawn with my arms cut, my neck burned, and my face looking like it was used as a punching bag." He sighed. "I think I'm sleepwalking again. Haven't done that since I was little. I have to try to function all day at school. A principal's job is never done."

"Can we do anything for you?" asked Penelope, feeling horrible for the man. It was clear he'd had an incredibly rough night, and if she was correct, he was now headed toward the high school for work. He'd no doubt be the talk of the teenagers of Everlasting for the day.

He shook his head. "I'll be fine. Just a bit banged up. I probably fell down my stairs at home while sleepwalking. That will teach me."

Petey grunted. "It looks like you fell down more than one flight and then wrestled with a bear. Oh, and the bear won."

"Feels like it too," said Sigmund, his expression slack. Waking up in such a condition would make anyone worry. "Have either of you seen Curt or Hugh? This morning I saw I had several phone messages from them last night, sounding frantic, but I haven't been able to reach either of them. Curt is sometimes a slow riser, but Hugh is always up at the crack of dawn. And no matter what they both answer their phones. Can't get in touch with Jake either."

Petey glanced at Penelope, his eyes widening. "Looks like they're all together hunting the thing that attacked you and Hugh."

It was Sigmund's turn to sound shocked. "Wait. What happened? Who attacked you? Are you okay? Is Hugh all right?"

"Everyone lived. They were out near the cliffs on the *Mary Marie* last night, and a kraken tried to eat them," said Petey. "And the night before I caught me a giant squid outside the Magic Eight Ball, but it wasn't there come morning. The thing was wearing a wristwatch. I remember that much."

Sigmund's expression lightened, and Penelope thought he'd laugh at Petey's ramblings. He didn't. "A wristwatch, huh?"

"Yep. Reminded me of the one your father had that he passed down to you before he died," said Petey, his features softening. "Strangest thing."

Sigmund perked, his attention held. "My watch went missing within the last week. I've looked all over town for it, but haven't been able to find it. And for the life of me I don't recall where I had it on at last. That is why I was reaching out to Jake this morning. I wanted to see if anyone had turned it in to the local lost and found."

Petey rubbed his arms absently. "This town is going to hell in a handbag. We should talk to Sheriff Bull about the rise in crime. Next you know, we'll be needing bars on all our windows and to hire ninjas to guard the town."

"Ninjas?" asked Penelope. Everlasting's surprises never seemed to end. "Are they real too?"

Petey gave her a side-eyed look. "Of course ninjas are real. Didn't they teach you anything in history class? Ninjas helped us win the American Revolution."

"Petey, there were no ninjas in the American Revolution," returned Penelope.

The older man stamped his foot much like a child having a tantrum. "Was so!"

She did her best to keep her face calm and her voice even. "Then why aren't they recorded in history books?"

"Pfft, because you can't see a ninja. If you see a ninja, then they're not very good at being stealthy, and that would mean they're not a real ninja. They tell me you're some big-city antiques seller. I figured you'd be smart enough to know ninjas are never seen."

Sigmund offered a warm smile, and Penelope was struck again with how handsome the man was. Everlasting sure didn't suffer from a shortage of good-looking men. "Sorry for him. It sounds like you've been made aware of Everlasting's secret. Let me guess, your grandfather told you everything."

"Hugh spilled the beans," said Petey. "Told her everything. He's in *love*. It will make you do foolish things. Trust me, I know. I'm an expert on the subject."

Sigmund and Penelope shared a look and each did their best to avoid laughing at the man.

"I hope you're here for longer than just a visit, Penelope," said Sigmund, lifting his book. "You're good for Hugh."

Grinning, she stepped closer to hug him. The minute she put her arms around him, the crystal Polly had given her began to glow and then heat.

One second she was hugging Sigmund, and the next, she and Sigmund were flat on their backsides on the sidewalk. It had felt like someone had taken a bat to her chest. Rubbing it, she looked to find Sigmund doing the same, his eyes wide.

"What was that?" he asked as he winced.

She shook her head, unsure what had happened. "The necklace Polly gave me started to glow, got hot, and then bam, it knocked us apart."

Groaning, Sigmund got to his feet as Petey helped her to hers. Sigmund touched his chest once more. "Packs a wallop, doesn't it?"

It sure did.

She lifted the necklace away from her and held

it out as far as it would go while still around her neck. "Why on earth did it do that?"

"It didn't want you hugging Sigmund. Hugh is going to want you wearing that all the time if it comes in a Curt-repellent form," said Petey, as if nothing out of the ordinary had just happened. Maybe, in his world, this was a totally normal occurrence.

"I hope it's not Petey repellent," she said with a wink.

Petey turned and grabbed Penelope, giving her a giant hug that smelled like whiskey. The necklace didn't respond in any way. "Yep. It's just Sigmund."

She sighed, confused as to what had occurred. "Or whatever happened was a fluke."

Petey eased the necklace from her neck and then thrust it at Sigmund. "One way to find out."

The necklace began to glow again and it pushed the two men apart with a force that stunned Penelope. Rushing forward, she snatched the necklace from Petey's hand and held it behind her back.

Petey smiled. "See. It's just Sigmund."

"No more tests," she said sternly.

Sigmund's eyes were wide. "I agree. I wonder why it has issue with me."

"I don't know," said Penelope. "I'm so sorry. I didn't know it would do that. You're banged up enough and here we are making matters worse. Please accept my apologies. When I see Polly again,

I'll try to get to the bottom of it. In the meantime, I won't be wearing the necklace."

"No worries," replied Sigmund as he bent to retrieve the book he'd been holding before getting knocked onto his backside. "I've got to be on my way. My allergy meds only last so long and then I'll be sneezing too hard to read the morning announcements over the PA system at school. Have Hugh call me when you see him."

"Will do," said Petey.

They continued on their way, and Penelope felt as though she'd actually tumbled down the rabbit hole. "Everlasting is so bizarre."

"Nah," argued Petey. "It's just like every other town that is full of supernaturals."

"There are more than one?" she asked in stunned disbelief.

"Of course. There are towns all over the world like Everlasting. It's common for like to attract like. We flock to areas with other supernaturals. Pretty natural. Some big cities are filled to the brim with supernaturals and humans are none the wiser for it. For the best. Humans like to panic. Skittish bunch, aren't they?"

He kept walking and she followed. Soon they were at the marina. They walked past the fishing charter building, past Curt's restaurant and then in the direction of a path that weaved through tall grass. Penelope drew to a stop as the path opened to show a magazine-worthy home near a rocky edge. The ocean was close and there was a small dock there. No boat was parked in the spot. The house itself was large, covered in medium-gray shaker-styled shingles and white trim. It looked as if someone had taken great pains to be sure it fit with the feel of New England's architecture. There was a rustic charm to it that was undeniable, and everything on it looked pristine.

Petey thumbed toward it. "Hugh's place."

"Wait, he lives there?" she asked, completely swept up with the home. It had everything down to a small white picket fence. There was an English garden planted out front that appeared to have been tended regularly and a wraparound deck with four oversized, white Adirondack chairs. The decking was built against the large home in a way that would give anyone sitting on it a glorious view of the water, along with a breezy spot to sit and enjoy the day.

The front door, which looked to lead to a sunporch, was bright red. Penelope couldn't believe how adorable the home was. She'd always dreamt of living in a house just like the one before her. It was as if Hugh had read her mind, even down to the carefully placed stepping-stones leading to the deck stairs.

It was truly breathtaking, and wasn't what she expected when she thought of Hugh. There was a wildness to him. Something that seemed so untamable and slightly feral. Yet everything about the cottage screamed order, serenity, and attention to details.

She thought about being on his sailboat. Nothing had been out of place. He was tidy and orderly. Nothing like her at all.

Petey grinned at her. "Weren't expecting this out of him, were you?"

"No," she breathed, still stunned the home belonged to Hugh. For some reason, she didn't picture him having something such as the home before her. But the harder she looked at it, the more she could see him there. "Did he inherit this?"

"Pft, no. Hugh built this place himself. The land was something he picked up when he bought out the previous owner of the fishing charter and boating tour place. This house was here, but it was rundown, about half the size you see now, and in complete disrepair. Hugh spent years renovating and expanding it, living at first off his boat before finally moving in here. Curt, Sigmund, and I helped where he'd let us with the rebuild, but Hugh prefers working alone."

"It's amazing," she said in a hushed tone.

"So is Hugh," added Petey. "He takes me down to the Keys during the snowiest months here, but I know he doesn't like leaving Everlasting. He runs a smaller fishing outfit down in the Keys during that time, and then has people running it for him the rest of the year while he's back here in Everlasting. This town is in his bones. If he wasn't always worried about me, he'd stay here year-round."

She grinned at the knowledge Hugh put Petey's needs before his own. There was also the fact the man was clearly good with his hands and talented. She couldn't even hang a picture and Hugh had managed to build a home that looked like it should be featured on the front of a home magazine. "Did he build those chairs on the porch?"

"He built everything, even down to his bed. He has a lot of energy and doesn't much like running with the local pack, so he channels that into something else," said Petey with a steadfast nod. "I tell him all the time that he should consider opening a shop in town to sell his furniture, or even talk to your grandfather about putting some pieces up there at his place. He doesn't think he's good enough to do that, and until you, he wouldn't even get near the antiques shop."

"His craftsmanship is amazing, and I've only seen a small sample of his work. I know that people in Chicago would pay big money for pieces like those," she said, pointing to the chairs on the porch. It was true. The chairs would easily go for three hundred each. Maybe more with the right buyers. It was hard to find pieces made that sturdy that looked that great. Hugh was exceptionally gifted.

Petey put his thumbs in his front pockets and

rocked in place. "Hugh doesn't believe me when I tell him he's talented. I blame that on his father. The man is one of those types that rarely has an encouraging word for another. Hugh spent his life being subjected to that. Tends to make one question their worth."

"Is Hugh close to his parents?" she inquired, feeling like she was intruding on Hugh's privacy, but curious all the same. She couldn't remember much of him from when they were younger.

"His father still lives in town, but on the other side, out near the forest. He bought up a bunch of land when Hugh was young. His mother passed when he was little. That was when his father moved him out to all that land. Hugh used to ride his bike into town and down here to the marina when he was in junior high so he could work on the docks, helping clean fish that tourists caught. He saved every penny and by the time he was in high school, he was running fishing charters for the previous owner. Hugh was a natural with customers and has always been able to read the sea—finding the sweetest honey holes to fish from."

Penelope let the man's words sink in. Hugh's mother had passed when he was young too? He understood her pain better than most. And she felt for him, wishing he was before her so she could wrap her arms around him and tell him he was important, talented, and worth something.

Shame on his father for not making sure the man knew as much.

Petey stared at her, sorrow coating his face. "Hugh and his momma were close. He loved her and would have done anything for her. Her passing hit him hard, and it drove an even bigger wedge between him and his father. There are rumors floating about town that some extended family to the Messings were responsible for her death. I don't how much truth is in that. I was near the market after lunch and heard some folks talking about how you hit Hugh with a semi on the highway this morning, so take everything you hear with a grain of salt. So I don't know if the Messings had anything to do with Hugh's mother's death or not. His momma and yours were friends and your mother wouldn't have let anyone hurt her."

"He didn't tell me that." Penelope's heart wrenched at the thought that anyone related to her, distant or not, could have harmed Hugh's mother. It made sense why Hugh seemed to harbor so much anger at her grandfather, and why he'd been reluctant to enter the antiques shop to begin with. He'd probably spent his life being told Grandpa Wil was the boogieman. Part of her began to wonder if it was true. Was the sweet, gentle soul who took the utmost care with precious antiques capable of great darkness?

Everything she'd thought she'd known about the

world had tipped upside down in a short period of time. She wasn't sure of anything anymore.

"Wouldn't think he would share that about his past," said Petey with a sigh. "He doesn't much like talking about it."

"Is he close with his father at all?" she asked, still soaking in the beauty of the home before her.

"No. Not a bit. His father is big into pack politics and Hugh couldn't care less about all that hogwash," supplied Petey, going to the gate of the fence. He opened it. "Hugh's father wanted him to be a lawyer like him, but Hugh had a love of the sea, like his momma did. The fishing charter was something he opened in memory of her. His father said he'd fail before the end of his first year—like so many start-up businesses do. Hugh proved him wrong. He makes a ton with his fishing charters and boat tours. Tourists eat it up. And he never stopped thinking of his mother. The sailboat he took you out on is named the *Mary Marie*. That was his mother's name."

Penelope teared up, and had to fight to keep from outright crying. Her alpha wolf-shifter really was a big softy, and she loved that about him.

Mine? Love?

Gasping, she took a small step back, her hand going to her chest as she realized just how deep her feelings ran for Hugh. She was in love with him. How was that possible?

It's fate.

She knew it was true. She loved the fish-stick-swearing, wolf-shifting fisherman.

Petey watched her and then winked. "Pretty sure he feels the same way about you. After what you told me about that kraken attack, my money is on him being out there hunting it. It's not in his nature to leave this be. If I'm right, he's doing so with your grandfather, and for Hugh to team up with Wilber for anything, it has to be for someone special."

A tear escaped and fell down her cheek. She wiped it away quickly.

The next thing she knew, Petey was there, blubbering, pulling an old handkerchief from his pocket and blowing his nose. He sounded like a foghorn. He sucked up his tears and then offered her the used handkerchief.

She cringed. There was no way she was touching that. "Um, thank you but I'm good."

He sniffled and then used the same handkerchief to wipe his eyes. "A good love story gets me every time. I'm a sympathetic crier. Drives Hugh nuts."

She laughed through her tears. "I bet it does. Don't worry, Petey. When I'm around, you won't be the only one crying."

He beamed. "That mean you're planning on staying in town?"

She hesitated. Was she? The idea of calling

Everlasting home felt right, but did she dare give up everything she had worked so hard for? If she did, would it be for the right reasons or because she was on the rebound after having her heart broken?

You never really loved Craig.

"You look lost in thought," said Petey.

"I'm really confused."

"It is what it is," offered the older man. "Fighting it is pointless. Go with what was destined, or forever swim against the current."

The man may use whiskey as cologne, but he was wise and he had a point. Life was short, and she'd wasted the last two years on a man who didn't appreciate her and never fully understood her or her oddities. Chicago was nice, but outside of work, she didn't socialize. Everlasting was charming, quaint, full of magic and wonder (just ask Polly), and her grandfather was here.

She didn't know if she had a future with Hugh. While she wanted to believe they were meant for one another, the skeptical side of herself wanted to protect her heart.

Petey pointed in the other direction, pulling her attention to the area. "There is a small cabin just down a bit. I live there. It's on Hugh's property. He won't let me pay any rent. Says that family takes care of family. I never had a family of my own. Hugh is the closest thing to a son I have. He's got some rough edges but a big heart. He'll do right by you, Penelope."

"This is all so sudden," she whispered.

Petey grunted. "Not for Everlasting. Normal rules don't apply here. The sooner you realize that, the sooner you can get on with being happy."

Unable to help herself, she pulled the man into a hug and held him tight. She kissed his cheek, ignoring the heavy smell of whiskey. When she drew back, his eyes held unshed tears. If he cried, she'd join in and it would be an endless cycle of tears.

He patted her arms and then stepped away from her, heading up the small walking path to the home. Penelope remained close at his heels. She glanced out at the water, wondering where Hugh was, and if he and her grandfather were really doing what Petey thought they were—hunting the kraken.

Worry churned in her stomach.

Petey stepped onto the deck and went for the wooden door. He opened it and let himself in as if he did so all the time. Reluctantly, Penelope followed. He chanced a glance back at her and grinned, showing off his missing tooth. "Come on in. Hugh won't mind. He doesn't even lock his doors."

She'd noticed as much.

Guess when you're able to shift into a wolf, you don't really worry about safety. You can eat whoever bothers you.

They entered onto a large three-season porch

that had two of the many front-facing windows propped open, letting some air through, but not enough to make the porch too chilly in the October air. The entire porch area was painted white. There was an oversized porch swing hanging by thick ropes, suspended from the ceiling. The swing was so big that it took her a moment to realize a twin mattress was its cushion. Royal blue and light blue throw pillows lined the back of it, giving a soft spot to lean against when sitting there. White chairs flanked each side of the swing. A lone blue pillow rested on each chair. There was a baby-blue throw over one chair back. A white wood coffee table sat in the center of the porch area. On it was a book about sailing and a small stone statue of a seagull.

A smile touched her lips. Hugh had done all of this himself? He wasn't just a talented furniture builder, he was also skilled with interior design. She bet he wouldn't want that advertised anywhere. It might hurt his manly imagine. She thought it was wonderful.

Her excitement didn't wane when they entered the main portion of the house. The living room area had a giant brick fireplace on a wall that was also brick. The wall had been left unpainted while the rest of the room was done in a soft gray. Two full sofas sat facing one another with a reclaimed-wood coffee table between them. On the table sat a small wooden lighthouse that looked remarkably like the lighthouse she'd been at and nearly asked directions from.

"Did he carve that?" she asked, pointing to the figure.

Petey grinned from ear to ear. "That is my handiwork. It was my housewarming present to Hugh. He does so much for me the least I could do was make him that."

"Oh my stars, Petey, it's beautiful and looks just like the one on the edge of town."

Beaming, Petey nodded. "Sat out there myself while I was making it. It was a way to give a gift to Hugh while also keeping an eye on my woman."

Confused, Penelope stared at him. "I'm afraid I'm not following."

He gave her a serious look. "Polly has a thing for Cornelius. He's bound to the lighthouse, so she goes out there a lot trying to see him. Sometimes I take her out when her car is acting up. Even got her a sidecar for my motorcycle. She has a shiny pink helmet. Her niece Anna says we're a menace on the road, but we don't agree. Oh, and Polly got me a shiny tiny disco ball for my key chain. We've matching ones. It practically means we're committed. It's like a promise ring, but not."

She wasn't sure the matching key chains meant what Petey thought they did, but she didn't want to burst Petey's bubble. He seemed happy and that was all that mattered. "Do you have eyes for anyone else? Besides Polly?"

Petey rubbed his jaw. "Nah. I like the chase with Polly. It's part of the charm."

Penelope grinned.

"Come on, I'll put on some tea for us while we wait for Hugh and your grandfather to get back," said Petey, walking down a hall in the direction of what she assumed was the kitchen.

Chapter Twenty-Two

Hugh headed into his house and instantly caught scent of Penelope. His body tightened with need and he hurried in. He found Petey in the kitchen, washing dishes, but there was no sign of Penelope.

Petey faced him. "Did you catch it?"

"No," breathed Hugh, still positive he could smell Penelope. "I'm heading to Wilber's. I want to check on Penelope. Buster is supposed to be watching over her."

"He called, frantic because she wasn't there when he woke," said Petey, moving to dry the dishes he'd just washed.

The air left Hugh's lungs as every worst-case scenario raced through his head. He turned, his intention to shift forms and run right to Wilber's shop if he had to. He needed to lay eyes on his woman and know she was safe.

"Slow yourself there, boy," snapped Petey. "She's resting up in your room. I made her something to eat and it became clear she was exhausted. I didn't give her any choice. I made her take a nap."

"She's here?" Hugh asked. "How?"

"I ran into her at the coffee shop and she asked me to walk her to the marina. She was looking for you. I didn't want to leave her alone with everything that's been happening, so I brought her here, to your place. Figured you'd want that."

Hugh went right at the older man and gave him a big hug, lifting Petey off the floor nearly a foot. He set him down and then nodded his thanks, unable to form the words.

Petey grinned. "She's a fine mate, Hugh. The two of you will have good-looking babies. I'll expect them to call me grandpappy. Got it?"

Having children hadn't been something Hugh had spent much time thinking about in the past. His father wasn't the best and Hugh had always held a hidden fear that he'd be the same way if he had children. That was why he'd always pushed the idea of starting a family far from his mind. He'd never met a woman before Penelope that he'd wanted a life with—something more.

Petey was like family to him. He was like a crazy uncle and a concerned father all rolled into one. He'd learned to control his wolf because of Petey's help. And he'd made something of his life despite his father thinking it would never happen because of Petey's encouragement. Of course any children Hugh might have in the future would call the man grandpa. "You got it, Petey."

"You going to claim her?" questioned Petey, putting two plates away in the cabinet. He knew that Hugh got antsy when anything was out of place. "And have you discussed it with her grandfather? I don't want your pelt on his wall."

Chuckling, Hugh inclined his head. "I informed him of my intentions while out to sea with him."

Petey snorted. "Brave man or very stupid. You're lucky he didn't use you to try to chum the waters for the kraken."

"I know. Trust me, I know." Hugh had been worried about extended time with Wilber, but in truth, he was finding the man wasn't quite the boogieman he'd always made him out to be. Sure, Wilber was no choirboy, but maybe he really had changed for the better. He hadn't actually hurt Jake when he'd kidnapped him. Something told Hugh that the Wilber of old would have killed Jake and been done with it from the start.

Progress.

It was slow but there.

Petey set the towel down. "I'm going to go check on that Pearson boy I hired to run my bait shop in the mornings. That boy spends more time reading those Japanese comic books than he does helping customers. And he doesn't know a bucktail jig from a flutter jig."

Hugh refrained from laughing. There had been a point in his life when he didn't know the difference either. Petey had been patient with him, showing him the fishing ropes. He'd do the same with the Pearson boy. As much as the man pretended to be hard-nosed, his heart was big. "I'm sure you'll set him straight."

Petey gave a curt nod. "I'll show him where a bear goes in the woods."

Hugh snorted. "You do that. Just do me a favor. Go easier on the whiskey. I'd like to have you around a long time, okay?"

"Can do."

"You could always switch to water," suggested Hugh, hopeful he'd finally talk some sense into Petey about his love of the hard stuff.

Petey looked aghast. "People drown in that, you know."

"Rome wasn't built in a day," said Hugh more to himself than Petey as he thought of the uphill battle he had to get Petey on the straight and narrow.

"Did you know ninjas helped build Rome?" said Petey, his expression serious.

Hugh had learned long ago to avoid trying to reason with Petey when he got on a ninja kick. "I think I heard about that."

"Yeah. Might want to talk to your woman. She

seems to think they didn't have a hand in the American Revolution. She's a sweet girl, but pretty misguided."

Hugh coughed. "I'll, um, let her know the real truth of it all."

"She's been fed and well taken care of. Don't go messing anything up by talking too much. Your foot likes to get stuck in your mouth."

Hugh grinned. "Thanks, Petey."

"No problem. Call me if you need me." With that, Petey headed out the back door.

Hugh went upstairs and discovered Penelope resting peacefully on his king-sized bed. Her long dark hair was fanned out around her on the white pillow and she had a gray throw blanket over her. Her boots were near the foot of the bed.

The longer he stared at her there, sleeping peacefully, the more he wanted to wake up every morning to that sight. He wanted her close and with him for the rest of his days. And while he'd already announced to her grandfather and his friends that he was going to ask her to be his wife, he had yet to figure out the best way to go about it all. It wasn't as if he had any practice.

He'd never even had a serious relationship. He had nothing more than a long line of one-night stands, and while he'd taken great pride in that knowledge before meeting Penelope, he found himself embarrassed by it now. If he could erase his past he would, but he couldn't. It was there to serve as an ugly reminder of who he no longer wanted to be.

He wanted more from life.

He wanted Penelope.

It no longer mattered that she was a Messing. She was his destined mate, and that meant the world to him. He wanted to crawl under the covers and join her. Touch her, know every inch of her, but he resisted. He needed a shower to wash away the smell of the chum they'd used to try to bait the kraken.

Without wasting another minute, Hugh made his way quietly across his bedroom to the large bathroom. He closed the door and then made short work out of cleaning up. He didn't want to waste another second of his life.

The hot water felt good sluicing over his sore muscles. His leg still had the smallest of cramps in it, from having been broken the day before when he'd gotten hit by the car.

A smile touched his lips as he thought about how he'd been reintroduced to Penelope. He'd been truthful when he'd told her hitting him with a car was the only way to knock sense into him. His stubborn side was notorious.

Stepping out of the shower, Hugh reached for the large bath towel he kept on a hook on the wall. Just as his fingers made contact with the fluffy towel, the bathroom door opened. Turning, he found Penelope there, her blue eyes wide, her jaw open and red stealing its way up her neck to her face.

"Hold the pickles, you're naked!" she yelped before spinning and putting her back to him. "I'm sorry. I didn't know you were home yet. I dozed off and oh my word, you're naked."

Covering himself with the towel, Hugh smiled. "I'm decent now."

She stayed facing the other way. "Pretty sure that subject is not only debatable but had a bet wagered on it."

"Penelope, really, I'm covered now." He wasn't sure how he felt about his mate refusing to see him without clothes on.

She gulped and stepped forward. "I should, um, do something. I'm not sure what because my brain is soup right now. Men should not come looking the way you do. It's like walking sin. Really wet, muscle-bound sin too."

He walked up behind her and bent, planting a kiss on her shoulder as she faced away and he held his towel. "I think you're downright sinful and you're fully dressed. In my book, women should not come as tempting as you are."

She turned slowly to face him. Confusion knit her brow. "You think I'm tempting?"

The sincerity on her face got his dander up. He

knew then that her ex Craig had done a number on her. He growled and then went to walk around her.

"What are you doing?" she asked.

"Calling your grandfather," he returned, heading to the phone by the side of the bed. "He and I are planning a road trip to break Craig's legs."

She was suddenly behind him, tugging on his upper arms. "No you don't. Find something else to bond with my grandfather over. Beating up my ex isn't on the list."

"It's on *my* list," he said, anger still coursing through him. "You're so beautiful that I want to pinch myself to be sure you're real, yet you don't seem to see it. I blame that worthless piece of pumpkin pie you were dating."

Penelope laughed.

Try as Hugh might, he found he couldn't cling to his anger for long. He chuckled too. "I really hope Polly's spell wears off soon. Baked goods are starting to sound dirty to me."

She ran her hands down his arms, making him shiver in delight. She then kissed his bare back. "Maybe we could do something about that."

Hugh froze. "Penelope?"

She nipped lightly at his skin and his shifter side went wild. He nearly lost control then and there. "We should put distance between us. I'm afraid I can only be a gentleman for so long."

"Hugh?"

"Yes?" he asked, his throat suddenly dry at her closeness.

"Stop being a gentleman and show me what a beast you can be," she said, turning him to face her. She went to her tiptoes, her lips finding his, and he knew the time had come to claim his mate.

Chapter Twenty-Three

Penelope woke late in the day to find the sun was already setting. She touched her neck and smiled at the thought of how she'd spent her day—with Hugh. It had been magical.

At one point, literally.

When he'd bitten her and said the word "mine," it had felt like their souls were being tied together. She'd then felt compelled to say the word back to him, making the feeling of soul sharing intensify.

She found her clothing and dressed before leaving the main bedroom and entering the upstairs hallway in search of Hugh. He'd been missing from the bed when she'd woken.

Catching the faint sound of voices coming from downstairs, she headed for the staircase. The voices were muffled at first, growing with intensity the farther down the stairs she went. She could make out Deputy March, Curt, Hugh, and then others. Whatever they were discussing had become heated rapidly, thus causing their voices to rise.

When she heard her grandfather's voice among the chaos, she quickened her pace. Hugh's home was large, and she worried that a fight would break out before she got to them.

She entered the kitchen to find Hugh and her grandfather standing toe to toe. Curt grabbed for Hugh, and Deputy March went for her grandfather as Petey put his body between both men.

"No killing each other," said Buster from the sidelines, looking like he wasn't about to try to get between anyone.

Penelope stepped into the kitchen and all eyes went to her. "What's going on here?"

Deputy March snorted. "Shock of all shocks, Wil and Hugh are at it *again*. I should have known when Hugh called us over to discuss tonight's hunt that all hell would break loose. Honestly, I'm the one who should want to start a fight with Wil because he kidnapped me. Yet here I am, playing peacemaker —again." It was strange seeing Deputy March in everyday clothing. There was still an air of danger to him that didn't lessen with the uniform missing.

Curt gave her a pleading look. "Can you tell them to stop acting like children?"

Her grandfather turned his gaze to her. "He claimed you?"

Unsure what that meant, she just stood there, staring at all the men before her. "Uh?"

"I did," said Hugh, answering for her. "It's done. She's my wife now. Deal with it."

Wife?

Penelope put her hands up, making the shape of a T. "Hold the pickles. Wife?"

Buster eased his way around the edge of the kitchen, bumping into the table as he did. A salt-shaker tipped over and he grabbed for it, keeping it from falling to the floor. Nervously, he set it back in place and then continued around the edge of the kitchen, in her direction. When he reached her, he leaned and lowered his voice. "The claiming ritual left the two of you mated. In the eyes of our people, you're now husband and wife."

"Claiming ritual?" As the words left her mouth, she remembered Hugh biting her neck during the height of passion. She touched the spot that was totally healed over as if nothing had happened. Her eyes narrowed on Hugh. "Start talking, bucko."

Gulping, he stopped trying to go at her grandfather and began a quick retreat. He ended up behind Curt. He glanced around the man who was a match to him in size and build. "You're adorable when you're mad. Don't geld me."

"*I'll* geld you," said her grandfather, making a move at him.

It took Jake, Curt, and Petey to pull him back.

Penelope came to her senses. "Stop!"

Everyone stopped in place like a game of freeze tag on the playground. She pointed to her grandfather. "You, go stand over there and stop trying to maim my boyfriend."

"Husband," reminded Buster before skulking away.

Her gaze whipped to Hugh, who was still acting like a giant baby and hiding behind his friend. "Explain this to me before it's me shoving my sunflower up your whoops-a-daisy."

Deputy March and Curt snickered.

Hugh paled as he took the smallest of steps out from behind Curt. "Honey, listen, don't be mad."

"Want me to kill him?" asked her grandfather, a hopeful note to his voice. "I'll do it. Say the word, sweetheart."

"No comments from the time-out corner," she said in her grandfather's direction. "Am I really married to Hugh now?"

"Unfortunately," stated her grandfather. "I really wish it would have been Curt."

"Again with the love and support, Gramps," said Hugh before snapping his mouth shut quickly.

Her hands went to her hips. "You should have asked me first. Before just up and claiming me. I didn't fully understand what was happening."

The look on Hugh's face said it all (she'd been more than on board with what they'd spent the afternoon doing). She'd have been embarrassed if she wasn't so stunned by the news they were now man and wife.

"I would have thought you'd have had the birds and the bees conversation by now," Hugh said with a wink.

Her grandfather stiffened.

Penelope pointed at Hugh. "You're on thin ice."

Curt smiled. "I've got this. You see, when a mommy bird meets a daddy bird and they—"

Penelope looked at her grandfather. "Okay, maim that one."

Curt's eyes widened. "I surrender!"

"Wimp," added Jake.

"I kind of like not being a rug," said Curt. He looked at Hugh. "You're on your own here. I know you love her and that it was fate, but she's right, a heads-up on it all would have been nice."

"Yeah, well you try to think clearly when love has your head spinning. Let's see how good you do," said Hugh with a grunt.

Penelope stiffened. "You love me?"

Hugh stared at her. "Of course I do."

"Why?" she asked.

He moved closer to her. "Because you have zero sense of fashion, you're quirky, sassy, love old things, can't drive worth a watermelon, and you naturally say silly things without a spell being cast on you. Oh, and you're easy on the eyes."

She stood there totally and completely shocked. He loved everything about her that Craig had loathed. The longer she stood there soaking in what Hugh had said, the more she began to tear up.

Petey was there, thrusting his used handkerchief at her, sniffling as he did. "Here. Tell the boy you love him too."

"My granddaughter does not love the previously foul-mouthed heathen," said Grandpa Wil.

Penelope locked gazes with Hugh. "I do love him. I don't know why. He is totally rough around the edges, has no filter, tends to let his temper get the better of him, and doesn't know how to look both ways before crossing a street. But he's also incredibly kind and caring, loves his friends like family, and would do anything for anyone. And," she winked, "he's not bad on the eyes either."

A lopsided grin spread over Hugh's face. "The way I see it, fate knew what it was doing in pairing us up. We could have spent months or years beating around the bush, but we didn't. We cut to the chase and made our future a reality. I love you, Penelope Lupine."

She tipped her head. "Lupine?"

"You're his wife and that means you get his last name," whispered Buster.

She squared her shoulders. "Not until he meets me in a church and does it proper. Until then, I'm a Messing on paper."

Hugh flashed a bad-boy smile. "I can live with that, so long as you agree to stay in Everlasting and live with me, as husband and wife."

Her grandfather grumbled.

She went to Hugh and tossed her arms around his neck, hugging him tight. "Fine, but you have to go to Chicago with me to help me move here."

"Done," he said.

Petey sniffled again, wiped his nose and then slid his handkerchief into the pocket of his overalls. He paused and then pulled out the necklace Polly had given her. "Oh, forgot I had this, Penelope. Here you go."

Grandpa Wil grabbed the necklace before she could take it. "Where did you get this?"

"Polly gave it to her," said Petey.

Grandpa Wil held up the necklace up. "Remember how I told you that long ago, hunters were given crystals to help them know who and what to hunt, and to protect them? This is one."

Penelope shook her head. "What? It's just a random necklace that Polly gave me right after she finished talking to her pet lobster. I don't think we can put a lot of stock in it."

"The necklace didn't like Sigmund giving her a hug today," said Petey. "It wasn't a fan of Sigmund at all. Lit up like the fourth of July then thrust him away. Poor guy already looked as if he'd been through a war. He had scratched-up arms and a burn on his neck. Not to mention a black eye."

Hugh gasped and grabbed Curt's shoulder, but looked at Grandpa Wil. "The kraken you hunted a century ago, was it from the Bails family?"

A hundred years ago?

Her grandfather was only in his early seventies.

"Come to think of it, yes, it was," said her grandfather, shocking her.

Curt's eyes widened. "You don't think Sigmund is the kraken, do you? He's our age and has never once shown any signs of shifting into anything."

"His mother is a were-shark, his father was a were-sea turtle, and his aunt can change into a dolphin. If anyone in this town was going to change into a kraken, it would be him," said Hugh, sounding like he didn't want his words to be true.

"But a kraken? Come on, those aren't common," argued Curt. "And he'd have shown signs earlier. We'd have known. He wouldn't have been able to keep that from us."

Deputy March grunted. "I'm betting he isn't even aware he's doing it."

Grandpa Wil sighed. "I heard Jolene mentioning a new medicine that Sigmund is on for his allergies. That might have very well triggered his shifter side. And since it's not second nature to him, being thirty, and having never shifted before, his body would fight it. My guess is the shift happens when he falls asleep."

"He thought he got banged up sleepwalking," said Penelope, unable to believe she was having a conversation about a man possibly turning into a kraken.

"And I saw a giant squid wearing his daddy's wristwatch, walking around town, in the direction of the marina," offered Petey. "Sigmund is the Kraken."

Deputy March glanced out the window. "If he is, he'll be shifting and heading to the water soon. We have to hurry if we want to stop him and keep him from killing anyone else."

"You can't kill him!" shouted Penelope.

The men all stared at her like she was nuts.

Curt lifted a brow. "We're going to keep him from going to the water and figure out a way to teach him control over his shifter side. We're not getting torches and pitchforks."

"I'm okay with pitchforks and torches," said her grandfather before grinning to show he was joking.

Chapter Twenty-Four

Hugh pulled his truck to a stop outside of Sigmund's house. Penelope and Petey exited his truck as well. Jake, Curt, Buster, and Wilber came to a screeching halt in Jake's SUV next to them. The moment everyone was out, they made their way toward Sigmund's front porch.

Jolene was there, sitting in a rocking chair, her hands folded on her lap. She didn't look the least bit surprised to see them.

"You knew?" Hugh asked.

With a nod, she stood slowly. She took a small step toward them and limped. "I figured it out the night of the storms. I was heading out on a call to give a tourist a tow and I saw Sigmund walking down the street in something like a trance state. I watched him partially shifting in the middle of the street before making his way in the direction of the water. I followed and tried to stop him but Petey happened on him."

Petey grunted. "Told everyone I saw a walking squid in a wristwatch."

Hugh ignored the man. "Jolene, why didn't you tell us? We could have helped."

"I was scared. Our family hasn't had a kraken-shifter in it in a hundred years. The last one we had was rotten to the core and killed for sport even when he wasn't shifted. My father told me that his father had sought out Wilber to help put a stop to it back then to prevent any more innocents from being killed. I went out into the ocean and tried my best to stop Sigmund, but he was stronger than me and ended up hurting me during the struggle. It's how I ended up with a sore ankle again."

Hugh sighed. "Sigmund isn't rotten to the core. He's the nicest guy I know and he hates violence."

She nodded. "I know. When he learns what he's done, he'll never forgive himself."

Wilber waved a hand dismissively. "He's nothing to feel bad about. I put some feelers out to my contacts about the two men found dead here. They were up to no good and here to hunt a centaur."

Jake stiffened. "W-what?"

Wilber nodded. "They were on the hunt for you. They planned to capture you alive if they could to sell to a collector. But from what I'm hearing, you'd fetch a good price dead too. Sigmund saved your life."

Jolene's eyes moistened. "But he attacked Hugh and Penelope on the boat."

Wilber stepped forward. "Jolene, he was more than likely trying to keep the two of them away from the cliff area. Those men weren't alone. And I think their secret meeting spot was near the cliffs. Sigmund may not have been thinking clearly as a kraken, but the man we all care for was in there enough to protect those he cares about."

"We're here to help him, not to hurt him," said Hugh, putting his hand out to Penelope. "We need him in one piece to tell him the good news."

"What good news?" asked Jolene, still looking as though she were on the verge of tears.

"Hugh and I are mated," said Penelope, smiling up at the woman.

Jolene cupped her mouth and tears began to fall. "I'm so happy for you two."

Petey rushed to her and held out his ever-ready handkerchief. He then stepped back and proceeded to cry along with Jolene.

Much to Hugh's amazement, it was Wilber who went to Jolene next and drew her into a hug. He held her and rocked her in place. "Shh, you don't need to carry this burden alone. We're all here now. We'll help Sigmund learn to control his shifter side."

Penelope tugged on Hugh's hand and he glanced down to find her crying too. "Honey?"

"I'm a sympathetic crier," she mouthed.

He snorted. "You're in good company with Petey nearby."

Jolene wiped her cheeks. "What will happen to Sigmund? Will you arrest him, Jake?"

Jake shook his head. "No. But I will take him with me for a few weeks, to some friends of mine who live down in Louisiana. They'll be able to help him learn to control his shifter side. And they'll help him process what he's done."

Chapter Twenty-Five

FOUR WEEKS LATER...

Penelope nudged Petey slightly, encouraging him to move forward. He'd been standing in the same spot out in front of Witch's Brew for nearly ten minutes. Grass would start to grow near his feet before he budged on his own.

When she'd cornered him and then talked him into a makeover, she never thought she'd find a man under all the fishing grime. She'd not only unearthed a man, but was surprised to find that Petey was handsome. He looked to be in his late seventies, but was strong as an ox and quick as a fox. From all that she'd learned about shifters from her husband, she knew Petey was far older than he appeared to be.

She'd also learned that Petey had turned down the opportunity to be a pack alpha, choosing instead to call Everlasting home. She didn't know how long he'd been a resident, but she did know that he'd been friends with Polly the entire time. He was sweet on Polly, but as far as Penelope knew, he'd never come right out and said as much to the eccentric woman.

That had been part of why Penelope had offered to help him with getting a haircut, shaving his scruffy beard, and dressing in something other than old overalls. If Petey was ready to make a move for Polly, then Penelope wanted to be as supportive as possible.

That had led them to be here, standing outside of Witch's Brew, as Petey tried to muster the courage to go forward with the plan. It had seemed clear-cut when they were at Petey's, putting the finishing touches together. They'd go to the flower shop, get Polly's favorite color flowers, and then Petey would go into the coffee shop, find Polly, and ask her out to dinner.

So far, all that had been accomplished was the flowers. Petey was doing his best to smash them to bits as he clutched them in a death grip. Petals fell to the sidewalk. Several landed on Petey's new dress shoes.

"Are you ready?" she asked for the fourth time since they'd arrived.

"I don't know about this, Penelope," he said, his voice cracking slightly. He reached for his finely combed hair that had taken Penelope a good hour to get to stay in place. As he ran his hand through it, messing it up slightly, she sighed.

He had on a blue long-sleeved shirt with a collar, a cream-colored sweater over it, along with a pair of tan slacks. The dress shoes she'd picked up for him looked great with the outfit, but he'd complained the entire way to the coffee shop about how they were pinching his toes and pointless in the real world.

Best of all, Petey no longer smelled of whiskey. Having known him a month, she now realized that he only drank the hard stuff while at the Magic Eight Ball. He carried whiskey with him at all times, using it like cologne. She wasn't sure why and gave up asking.

It had taken some doing, but she'd managed to talk him out of using whiskey as aftershave this morning. Instead, she'd gifted him a nice bottle of aftershave. It smelled great on him.

"You look so handsome, Petey," she said, touching his arm gently. "Polly is going to love it."

He held the bouquet of pink flowers so close to his chest that there didn't look to be one left intact. She took hold of his hands and walked around to face him, drawing his attention to her and from the coffee shop.

"Take a deep breath and relax," she soothed.

He did as instructed. "I can do this."

"Yes, you can."

"I just need to tell her how I feel about her. Easy as pie."

She smiled. "Yep."

The shop door opened and Polly walked out carrying a box of goodies. She was humming merrily to herself and smiled up at Penelope before walking onward.

She then stopped and pivoted around, dropping the box of goodies in the process, her eyes on Petey. "Petey?"

"Hi, Polly," he said sheepishly, holding what was left of the flowers out to her. "Here. These are for you."

She stood rooted in place, as something akin to horror washed over her face. "What happened to you?"

"Penelope," he said, as if that explained everything.

Polly's gaze whipped to Penelope. "You ruined him."

"Ruined?" asked Penelope, lost as to what the woman meant.

"Where are his favorite overalls? Where are his fishing boots? Where is his lucky knit cap? And why does he smell like that?" demanded Polly.

"Because I showered and shaved," said Petey, lowering his head. "Don't you want the flowers?"

Polly stepped over the box of baked goods on the sidewalk and went right for Petey. She reached up and tousled his hair, messing it up to the way it normally looked. "You were perfect before. I like you just the way you normally are. This version isn't you. We've been friends far too long for you to start putting on airs for me."

Penelope stood there at a loss for words. The woman actually liked the scruffy, unkempt fisherman who often smelled like he'd bathed at a distillery?

Polly tugged on Petey's shoulder, making him bend. When he did, she kissed his cheek lightly. "You don't need to change, Petey. I like you just as you are. I've never thought you needed to change."

Petey blushed. "Thanks, Polly."

Polly headed back for the box of baked goods, picked them up, and then glanced back at Penelope. "Thank you, but some things are just right without any tweaks. Now, I'm off to see a ghost—*hopefully*."

She hurried off, leaving Penelope standing there with Petey.

Hugh pulled up in his truck and parked. He got out, made his way around several tourists, and came right for her. "Hey, honey, how is the shop today? Your grandfather still peeking in to be sure he left instructions for everything or is he finally letting you run it now that he handed it over to you? For a man who is technically retired, he works nonstop."

She laughed. "I gave up today and let him go there. I had something else to do."

Hugh glanced fleetingly at Petey and then back at Penelope. "Mmm, what do you say to having lunch with your husband? I'm starving and spent the morning doing an extra charter. Petey never showed for work. That isn't like him."

Penelope grinned and pointed to Petey. "He's been with me."

Hugh looked toward Petey again and gasped. "Sweet buttery scones, Petey, is that you?"

Polly's spell had worn off several days prior, but Hugh had gotten so used to the sayings that he'd kept them.

"It is," said Petey, still holding the flowers that had been for Polly.

"You clean up nice," said Hugh with a laugh. "But you look uncomfortable."

"These shoes are killing me and this sweater itches," said Petey. "I look ridiculous. Penelope seemed so happy about it all that I didn't want to stop her."

Hugh wrapped his arms around Penelope and kissed her cheek. "Honey, I love that you made an effort with him, but he's an old dog and doesn't really like new tricks."

"He's not the only one," said Penelope. "Polly likes the fishing-gear version of him better."

Hugh laughed.

A group of tourists walked by. They were all women who were in their sixties. Each one was watching Petey. The woman on the end stopped and smiled sweetly at him. "Hello there."

Petey nodded. "Afternoon, ma'am."

Hugh put his lips to Penelope's ear. "Looks like other women find the new version of Petey attractive."

Petey stiffened, and Penelope realized with his wolf-shifter senses, he'd overheard Hugh. He cleared his throats. "Ladies, if you'll excuse me, I have to go find my woman and give her these flowers. I'm not about to let some old goat of a ghost steal her heart."

"Petey?" asked Penelope.

He smiled. "It's all about the chase."

He rushed off.

The women shared a look and then went into the antiques shop.

Hugh laughed. "They'll be hitting on Wilber next."

Penelope groaned. "I hope not. Eww. That is Grandpa we're talking about there. Besides, I think he's only got eyes for Jolene."

"Honey, how about we stay out of their love lives and focus on our own? They'll sort it out themselves." Hugh nuzzled his face to her neck. "Now, I'm going to take my wife to lunch. How does that sound?"

"Perfect," she said. "I'm starving. I've been craving pickles all morning."

Hugh squeezed her tight, his expression going blank. "You're craving pickles? You hate pickles."

"I know. It's weird. They're all I can think about," she said.

Hugh stared down the length of her. "You don't think you're pregnant, do you?"

She actually hadn't given that any thought.

Hugh lifted her, spun her in a circle and then set her down, grinning from ear to ear. "I'll call the doctor and get you an appointment for today. I can't wait. I hope it's a girl. I was a hellion and I don't know if I can handle a boy."

She laughed. "Feed me first and don't hold the pickles."

THE END

BE sure to watch for additional Everlasting books from Mandy M. Roth! Sign up for her newsletter today so you don't miss out on stories about Sigmund, Curt, Jake, or the devil—plus many more!

Newsletter

Want to be up to date on new books, new
audiobook & other fun stuff from Mandy?

Sign-up for Mandy's newsletter

About the Author

New York Times & *USA TODAY*
Bestselling Author

Mandy M. Roth is a self-proclaimed Goonie, loves 80s music and movies and wishes leg warmers would come back into fashion. She also thinks the movie The Breakfast Club should be mandatory viewing for...okay, everyone. When she's not dancing around her office to the sounds of the 80s or writing books, she can be found designing book covers for New York publishers, small presses, and indie authors.

www.mandyroth.com

Featured Titles from Mandy M. Roth

The Immortal Ops Series World
Immortal Ops
Critical Intelligence
Radar Deception
Strategic Vulnerability
Tactical Magik
Act of Mercy
Administrative Control
Act of Surrender
Broken Communication
Separation Zone
Act of Submission
Damage Report
Act of Command
Wolf's Surrender
The Dragon Shifter's Duty
Midnight Echoes

275

Isolated Maneuver

Expecting Darkness

Area of Influence

And more to come…

Tempting Fate Series

Loup Garou

Bad Moon Rising (Coming Soon)

And more to come…

The Guardians Series

The Guardians

Crossing Hudson

Ruling Jude (Coming soon)

The Druid Series

Sacred Places

Goddess of the Grove

Winter Solstice

A Druid of Her Own

The King of Prey Series

King of Prey

A View to a Kill

Master of the Hunt

Rise of the King

Prince of Pleasure

Prince of Flight

Bureau of Paranormal Investigation (BPI)
Hunted Holiday

Heated Holiday

Pleasure Cruise Series
Pleasure Cruise

Date with Destiny

Pleasure Island

Prospect Springs Shifters
Blaze of Glory

Parker's Honor

Gabe's Fortune

The League of the Unnatural
Pike's Peak

Adam's Angel

Loving Lars (Coming Soon)

And more than this small sum up can contain! Visit Mandy M. Roth for a complete list of her titles! www.MandyRoth.com

More Everlasting...

COZY PARANORMAL MYSTERY ROMANCE NOVELS

The Happily Everlasting Series

Dead Man Talking
by Jana DeLeon

Once Hunted, Twice Shy
by Mandy M. Roth

Fooled Around and Spelled in Love
by Michelle M. Pillow

Witchful Thinking
by Kristen Painter

Visit Everlasting
https://welcometoeverlasting.com/

Dead Man Talking

by Jana DeLeon

Welcome to Everlasting, Maine, where there's no such thing as normal.

Meteorologist Zoe Parker put Everlasting in her rearview mirror as soon as she had her college degree in hand. But when Sapphire, her eccentric great-aunt, takes a tumble down the stairs in her lighthouse home, Zoe returns to the tiny fishing hamlet to look after her. Zoe has barely crossed the county line when strange things start happening with the weather, and she discovers Sapphire's fall was no accident. Someone is searching the lighthouse but Sapphire has no idea what they're looking for. Determined to ensure her aunt's ongoing safety, Zoe promises to expose the intruders, even though it means staying in Everlasting and confronting the past she thought she'd put behind her.

Dane Stanton never expected to see Zoe standing in the middle of her aunt's living room, and was even more unprepared for the flood of emotion he experiences when coming face to face with his old flame. Zoe is just as independent and determined as he remembered, and Dane knows she won't rest until Sapphire can return to the light-house in peace, so he offers to help her sort things out.

Armed with old legends, Sapphire's ten cats, and a talking ghost, Zoe has to reconcile her feelings for Dane and embrace her destiny before it's too late.

Once Hunted, Twice Shy

by Mandy M. Roth

Welcome to Everlasting, Maine, where there's no such thing as normal.

Wolf shifter Hugh Lupine simply wants to make it through the month and win the bet he has with his best friend. He's not looking to date anyone, or to solve a murder, but when a breath taking beauty runs him over (literally) he's left no choice but to take notice of the quirky, sassy newcomer. She'd be perfect if it wasn't for the fact she's the grand-daughter of the local supernatural hunter. Even if he can set aside his feelings about her family, Penelope is his complete opposite in all ways.

Penelope Messing wanted to get away from the harsh reminder that her boyfriend of two years dumped her. Several pints of ice cream and one plane ticket to Maine later, she's ready to forget her troubles. At least for a bit. When she arrives in the sleepy little fishing town of Everlasting, for a surprise visit with her grandfather, she soon learns that outrunning one problem can lead to a whole mess of others. She finds herself the prime suspect in a double homicide. She doesn't even kill spiders, let alone people, but local law enforcement has their eyes on her.

The secrets of Everlasting come to light and Penelope has to not only accept that things that go bump in the night are real, but apparently, she's destined for a man who sprouts fur and has a bizarre obsession with fish sticks. Can they clear Penelope's name and set aside their differences to find true love?

Fooled Around and Spelled in Love

---

by Michelle M. Pillow

*Welcome to Everlasting, Maine, where there's no such thing
as normal.*

Anna Crawford is well aware her town is filled with
supernaturals, but she isn't exactly willing to
embrace her paranormal gifts. Her aunt says she's a
witch-in-denial. All Anna wants is to live a quiet
"normal" life and run her business, Witch's Brew
Coffee Shop and Bakery. But everything is about to
be turned upside down the moment Jackson Argent
walks into her life.

Jackson isn't sure why he agreed to come back to
his boyhood home of Everlasting. It's like a spell was
cast and he couldn't say no. Covering the Cranberry
Festival isn't exactly the hard-hitting news this

reporter is used to. But when a local death is ruled an accident, and the police aren't interested in investigating, he takes it upon himself to get to the bottom of the mystery. To do that, he'll need to enlist the help of the beautiful coffee shop owner.

It soon becomes apparent things are not what they seem and more than coffee is brewing in Everlasting.

Witchful Thinking
_____

by Kristen Painter

Welcome to Everlasting, Maine, where there's no such thing
as normal.

Charlotte Fenchurch knows that, which is why she's not that surprised when a very special book of magic falls into her hands at the library where she works. As a fledgling witch, owning her own grimoire is a dream come true. But there's something...mysterious about the book she just can't figure out.

Leopard shifter Walker Black knows what's odd about the book. It's full of black magic and so dangerous that it could destroy the world. Good thing the Fraternal Order of Light has sent him to Everlasting to recover it and put it into safe storage.

If he has to, he'll even take the witch who owns it into custody.

That is until he meets Charlotte and realizes she's not out to watch the world burn. She's sweet and kind and wonderful. Suddenly protecting her is all he wants to do. Well, that and kiss her some more. But dark forces seem determined to get their hands on the book, making Charlotte their target, and Walker worries that he won't be able to protect her from them – or the organization he works for.

Can Walker and Charlotte survive the onslaught of danger? Or is that just witchful thinking?

Visit Everlasting

https://welcometoeverlasting.com/

CPSIA information can be obtained
at www.ICGtesting.com
Printed in the USA
LVOW11s1747060418
572581LV00002B/389/P